Tori Carrington

RECKLESS PLEASURES

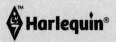 **Harlequin®**

TORONTO NEW YORK LONDON
AMSTERDAM PARIS SYDNEY HAMBURG
STOCKHOLM ATHENS TOKYO MILAN MADRID
PRAGUE WARSAW BUDAPEST AUCKLAND

Recycling programs
for this product may
not exist in your area.

ISBN-13: 978-0-373-79621-2

RECKLESS PLEASURES

ABOUT THE AUTHOR

Multi-award-winning, bestselling authors Lori Schlachter Karayianni and Tony Karayianni are the power behind the pen name Tori Carrington. Their more than forty-five titles include numerous Harlequin Blaze miniseries, as well as the ongoing Sofie Metropolis comedic mystery series with another publisher. Visit www.toricarrington.net and www.sofiemetro.com for more information on the duo and their titles.

Books by Tori Carrington

HARLEQUIN BLAZE

To get the inside scoop on Harlequin Blaze and its talented writers, be sure to check out blazeauthors.com.

Don't miss any of our special offers. Write to us at the following address for information on our newest releases.

Harlequin Reader Service
U.S.: 3010 Walden Ave., P.O. Box 1325, Buffalo, NY 14269
Canadian: P.O. Box 609, Fort Erie, Ont. L2A 5X3

We dedicate this book to readers like us who enjoy a healthy dash of the forbidden with their sex. And, as always, to editor extraordinaire Brenda Chin, who merely smiles when we come up with our outlandish ideas, her red pencil at the ready...

Prologue

Eighteen months…

MEGAN MCGOWAN LAZILY rubbed her calf against
Darius's leg and curved her body close against his,
finding it impossible to swallow the amount of time
he'd be away.

A year and a half…

Seventy-five weeks…

Five hundred and sixty-three days…

A long, long time until she'd be able to feel his
skin against hers again… His breath teasing her ear…
His thick, hard length stroking her wet softness…
Filling her… Making her whole…

"It's not like we haven't had time to prepare," Dari
whispered and then kissed her hair. "The order came
down months ago." He kissed her mouth, igniting in
her a desire to feel his skillful attentions directed
toward other more strategic areas of her anatomy.
"And we've both been here before."

She hummed, pressing her nose against his neck. "I know. But back then we were both shipping out. Now…"

She caught herself up short. Now she was like the spouse being left behind.

Only she wasn't a spouse. Not yet. Dari kept threatening to propose, and while they both joked about marriage, they were still very single. They even maintained separate apartments, although they mostly spent their time together at her place. Dari said it was because she was more likely to have something in the refrigerator; she knew it was because his place was more like a true bachelor pad, where he left his military neatness at the door.

They were both Marines. But where she had completed her tour of duty and accepted honorary discharge, Dari remained a reservist and thus could be called back at any time. And he had been.

"Would you feel better if you were being sent back out with me?"

She realized she would. "Yes."

And that knowledge helped her relax.

"You're good at that, you know," she said, kissing his neck, tasting the salt of his sweat there from their hours-long sack session.

"I'm good at everything."

She laughed. "I mean, you're good at telling me exactly what I need to hear, exactly when I need it."

She pulled back to look into his handsome face

draped in shadows. It would be dawn soon…and shortly after that she would drive him to Petersen Air Base where he would catch a ride on the first transport out.

"I try," he joked.

She smiled.

He kissed her leisurely. "I'm sure Lazarus will take a lot of your energy."

Lazarus Security.

In her vulnerable state, the name stirred emotions both of sadness and hope…and served to distract her, however briefly, from the other more pressing issues at hand.

Was it really over a year ago that their friend Barry Lazaro had surrendered to the ultimate enemy?

Still, it seemed impossible. He had survived so much while they were on the front lines overseas. He'd been the most capable of them, the go-to guy, the one to lead the charge… Ironic that returning to civilian life had proven the one battle he'd ended up losing. Lazaro had been home only a couple of months when he'd been found hanging from his own shower-curtain rod, dead.

Megan went still, the memory almost too much for her to handle just then.

It was in Barry's name the five surviving members of the elite team whose friendship was forever fused while fighting in Waziristan established Lazarus Security: her, Darius, Jason Savage, Lincoln Williams and Eli Stark.

Lord knew building the independent security company had taken all their energy over the past few months, along with the nonstop attention of the four active partners. She, Dari and Jason handled most of the organizational and grunt work. With his background in both the military and the FBI, Linc had the strong government ties that would bring in subcontract work normally seen to by active ranks. And Eli...

Well, Eli had taken the news of Lazaro's death the hardest, offering up the financial resources with which to start the company, but insisting he remain a silent partner.

Megan wondered if they'd all known, going in, how hard they'd have to work if they'd still have done it.

Then again, seeing as they were all either ex- or semiactive military, hard work was no stranger to them. And they were poised to make some major inroads in the industry, with plans that needed to be implemented, personnel hired, compound expansion overseen.

One day Lazarus Security would serve as the ultimate tribute to a fallen hero, a man they'd all known and loved.

"It won't be the same without you here," she whispered now to Dari.

He smoothed his hand over her hair and down her back, eliciting a delicious shiver that left her wishing his fingers even farther south.

"Don't you dare meet anyone else over there." Her words were barely audible, and so unlike anything she'd usually say, they surprised her.

But Dari seemed to take them in stride as he chuckled and easily slid her to lie on top of him, toe to toe, nose to nose, setting fire to every inch of her. "I have more than I can handle with you…."

He kissed her, much the same way he had the first time while they were stationed together in Afghanistan two years ago. The night had been cool and airless…the sex sweaty and hot. She hadn't been able to get enough of him then…and nothing had changed. No matter how often they made love, she wanted more.

She knew he wouldn't stray. It wasn't the way he was made. They didn't come any truer than Darius Folsom. It was the second thing she loved about him.

The first was how he touched her…

His fingers firmly budged in the direction she'd been craving, cupping her bottom then moving toward her shallow crevice. She caught her breath.

"How about you?" he asked.

She swallowed hard, barely able to concentrate over the rush of white-hot sensation. "Me?"

"Mmm…do I have to worry about you being here, all by yourself?"

His fingertips found her slick, swollen folds from behind. She automatically spread her thighs to allow him easy access, her heart beating heavily in her chest.

She searched his eyes. "I don't know. Do you?"

She flicked her tongue slightly inside his mouth and then withdrew it.

Before Dari, she'd never really been involved in a long-term relationship. Her love life had been dotted with temporary lovers, few of them lasting beyond the three-month mark. And none beyond six months.

Which made the longevity of their relationship all the more special….

And his leaving now all the more frightening…

"Yes, well, I've already asked Jason to keep an eye on you," he said, stealing her breath with a gentle pinch to her clit.

"Jason Savage?" she whispered, fighting to follow the conversation, even as she longed to feel him inside her again. Now.

"Uh-huh."

She'd known Jason almost as long as she had Dari. But the bond between the two men stretched back even further than that. The two Marines were cut from much the same cloth physically, but couldn't be more different emotionally.

Where Dari was steadfast, Jason roamed.

She placed her knees on either side of his legs and scooted until her heated folds pressed against his pulsing hard-on. "And you trust him?" she asked.

"He's been my best friend since I was five."

She rocked her hips, rubbing her wetness down

his thick length. "He also nails everything that moves."

Dari groaned at her movements, his expression going sober at her words. "Not my girl."

Funny how those three simple words always made her stomach flutter. It didn't matter that she was a Marine. Or that she saw herself as his equal. Whenever he laid claim to her, she felt like his girl.

He reached for a condom on the nightstand, quickly sheathed himself and then grasped her hips, entering her in one, long upward thrust that forced all thought from her mind. She moaned into his mouth, all too happy to welcome him into her body again… and again. As often as she could before time and space and the military would force them apart for eighteen long months.

1

Four months later...

MEGAN AIMED THE M-16 semiautomatic rifle at the man-size moving targets a hundred and fifty yards away, testing not so much her own acumen—she'd been a crack shot from the time she'd learned to shoot at ten and was a consummate pro now—but the quality of the exercise Lazarus staff had put together for trainees on the grounds just outside Colorado Springs, Colorado, a place none of them were from...but the place Barry Lazaro had called home.

"Still too slow!" she shouted toward the control booth.

She no sooner said the words than the target sped up and then slowed back down again. She missed.

Blowing a long breath between her teeth, she dropped the rifle to rest against her hips and stared at the control booth where Jason Savage grinned at her.

"You told me you wanted it faster."

"That I did."

She considered aiming the gun in his direction then thought better of it. A pro never turned her weapon on another unless she meant to shoot. And while the temptation was strong…

"We done for now?"

She nodded. "We'll make another assessment during the next training session."

She walked toward the main complex, let herself in and then entered the armory where she checked and cleaned the rifle before putting it away.

Lazarus Security was growing faster than any of them had dreamed. The property was spread over a hundred acres, the main compound positioned in the southwestern corner, twenty-five thousand square feet of a plain, square, one-story structure that boasted a full gym, firing range, classrooms, a fully stocked armory and even a barracks that held twenty bunks, should the need arise. Outside they had five different training courses, including a dirt track for bike training and a paved one to teach evasive maneuvers while driving.

Word had spread and they were having trouble keeping up with demand, bringing in fresh trainees every two weeks, most ex-military, which made them almost job ready.

Still, while contracts were rolling in, they were mostly of the low-caliber security-detail variety: bodyguards, drivers, installing home and business security systems. While none of the partners complained, Megan had hoped for something a little more...exciting.

She opened the armory door and nearly ran straight into Jason Savage.

He lifted his hands as if in surrender and chuckled. "I give up."

"Very funny," she said.

At just over six foot three, Jason was a little taller than Darius...and much darker. Where Dari had light brown hair and eyes, Jason's were almost black.

But the differences went beyond the physical: Jason was somehow also darker in demeanor. Something lurked beyond the surface, shadowy and dangerous.

Still, she'd be the first to admit surprise at the way he'd stepped up after Dari had shipped back out. She guessed it was because they were both being forced to go without someone important in their lives.

"Where you heading?" Jason asked.

She glanced at him as they walked, both of them dressed in training fatigues. "The front offices."

"Me, too. I'll walk with you."

They headed down the hall that would take them outside to a pathway leading to the public offices, each structure separate and secure from the next.

And miles apart in appearance.

"Still haven't heard from Dari, huh?" Jason asked as he opened the door and she passed through it.

Megan stared at him, blinking against the early-afternoon sunlight as they crossed to the more aes-thetically pleasing building that housed the main offices. It looked more like a small, modern home than a commercial structure.

Jason shrugged. "Hey, you're always a little more uptight when you're out of contact."

She grimaced, recognizing he probably was right. But it didn't make her feel any better to be called uptight.

"I haven't heard from him in two weeks," she admitted.

"Yeah, me, too. Field trip."

Field trip was code for extra-remote mission where an elite group was sent into a sensitive area and all contact with the outside world was off-limits unless they needed help from command.

Megan caught herself scratching her arm.

She was well versed on the life of a Marine. Hell, she was one herself, albeit retired, despite the saying that a Marine was always a Marine. But that hadn't made the past four months any easier. Especially now that Dari was out of contact. At least before, they'd been able to arrange the occasional video chat and had spoken on the phone a couple of times a week when their schedules meshed…and sexted like there was no tomorrow.

But now that he'd gone silent, she felt oddly as if the world had stopped spinning.

She and Jason entered the office building.

It always caught her off guard, moving from one

structure to the other. In her fatigues, she felt out of place in the nicely decorated, civilized surroundings; a sensation she didn't experience when she came in dressed to impress in client and business meetings.

"I guess this is where we part ways," Jason said, grinning. "I have a certain receptionist I need to charm."

Megan gave a surprised laugh and an eye roll. "If she's got half a brain, she'll shoot you down flat."

"Who said I was interested in her brain?"

She smiled. "Who, indeed."

She opened her office door.

"Hey," Jason called. "Why don't you stop by The Barracks later?"

Every day he extended the same invitation to drop by his favorite watering hole; every day she refused.

"Maybe," she said noncommittally.

"A step up from no," he said.

She supposed it was, but she wasn't entirely convinced…

MEGAN'S ONE-BEDROOM apartment on the west side of Colorado Springs had always seemed small, but ever since Dari had left, it felt somehow…too big.

It was eight-thirty and the sun was, for all intents and purposes, down, even though it was more blocked by the Rocky Mountains to the west than truly set. She lay across her double bed in one of the old denim shirts Dari had left behind, staring at the ceiling. She wondered what he was doing that moment. Was he navigating the remote region of Waziristan, seeking out enemies that knew the caves and rugged terrain better than he and his guys ever would? Was he camped out under the starry dome of the sky, one eye on the nearby hill where an enemy combatant could appear any moment?

Was he thinking about her?

She groaned and rolled over, burying her head in his pillow and breathing deeply.

She was pathetic.

Lord knew she had enough to occupy her time. Then why was she spending so much of it pining after a man who was already hers?

Because she missed him…with every fiber of her being.

She turned her head on the pillow and stared at her cell phone on the nightstand. The ringer was set to High in case he called. Still, she couldn't stop herself from reaching for the silent piece of technology and lighting the display: no calls, no messages, no texts.

She sighed heavily, suddenly aware of the rumbling of her stomach.

Had she eaten dinner? She couldn't remember. Probably not a good sign.

She tried to think of what she had in the kitchen and smiled. Dari would be amused that for the first time she didn't have much of anything in the refrigerator, solely because she was too distracted to think about shopping before coming home.

She forced herself from the bed and padded barefoot toward the room in question, hauling open the fridge door. Nothing but a half gallon of milk that held all of an inch worth of the liquid, a few wrapped slices of American cheese, a single serving of yogurt that had been in there for God only knew how long and the requisite condiment bottles.

She took out one of the pieces of cheese and unwrapped it, snacking on it as she closed the fridge door and checked out the cabinets. Not a thing she could use to fix herself a decent meal.

She thought of the delivery menus in the drawer… but usually the only time she ordered in was when Dari was over and they were too exhausted after sex to even make themselves a sandwich.

She smiled at the memory and then immediately grimaced.

"Oh, screw it."

She walked with purpose back into the bedroom, checked her still-silent cell and then got dressed…

MEGAN HADN'T BEEN to The Barracks in four months—not since the night of Dari's sending-off party. But the thought of spending one more night in her apartment by herself had chased her clean out. That the bar also served burgers was a bonus.

One good thing about a place like this was no matter how long you'd been away, they always remembered you. She caught at least four shouts out to her. She acknowledged them with a friendly smile, looking over what was a decent crowd for a Thursday night. A waving hand caught her attention at the end of the bar and she waved back at Jason.

"Up, Marine," he said to the young guy on the stool next to him when she stepped up.

Megan was amused by how fast the freshly returned Marine did as ordered. She half expected him to salute Jason, although she could have told him not to bother. Jason hadn't been honorably discharged; he'd been thrown out of the service and probably had a permanent outline of the boot mark on his behind.

"Thanks," she said to the Marine as she claimed the stool.

"What about me?" Jason asked with a raised brow before taking a long pull from his beer bottle.

"What? Why didn't I thank you?"

His grin widened.

"Well, it wasn't as if *you'd* given up your stool for me."

A couple of *ohs* and ribbing erupted among the others around them.

One of the females spoke up. "A woman expecting a man to give her his chair doesn't deserve one."

Megan flashed her a smile. "A woman stupid enough to refuse an offered chair should sit on the floor...or be hit upside the head with one."

More hoots.

And just like that, she reentered the swing of things, as if she'd been there a few days before instead of a few months.

She placed an order for whatever was on tap, along with a cheeseburger, hold the fries. Jason told the girl to add the fries.

After she left, Megan looked at him. "I hope you plan on eating them."

"I may have one or two," he said. "But my plan is to make sure you eat them. Dari's not going to be pleased when he hears you've dropped at least ten."

Twelve. But who was counting? She accepted the beer and took a nice long sip. "Don't tell me you guys actually waste time talking about me…"

When you talk. That's what she'd been prepared to say. Instead, she left the words drift off and took her cell phone out of her purse, placing it prominently on the bar in front of her.

"Are you kidding? If it were up to him, you would be the only thing we talk about."

"Yeah, and next you're going to try to convince me that the b.s. coming out of your mouth is actually the truth."

She'd meant the words as a joke. But as she looked at him, prepared for a funny comeback, she watched him take another drink from his bottle then run the back of his hand across his mouth, his eyes sober and observant, as if trying to figure something out.

"Are you serious?" She forced herself to laugh.

"As an IED."

She squinted at him.

Jason shrugged and faced the front of the bar. "I can tell you that he's probably going crazy right now not being able to talk to you."

She caught herself staring at her blank cell-phone display and looked away. Well, that made two of them...

"Come on. A great deal of your time has to be spent discussing Lazarus."

Jason slowly shook his head. "Nope."

She paused for a long moment, considering what the conversation between the two guys might sound like.

"He says he knows we'll take care of whatever needs taking over in that regard," Jason said.

Now that she thought about it, the words sounded like ones Dari would say. He was never one to worry about items over which he had no control. Besides, he probably had his hands full over there. He never shared details, even though she and Jason would not only understand, they'd empathize.

"Hey."

Megan glanced up from where she'd been staring at her silent cell again. Jason's younger brother, Jackson, wiped down the bar in front of her and then presented her burger. Jason automatically reached for a couple of fries and she slapped his hand away.

"Hey, yourself, Jax," she said. "You cook this?"

"Sure did."

She'd heard it said at the compound that Jackson

Savage had been by to apply for a job…and that his brother had refused him out of hand: twice.

"I was hoping you and I could talk sometime soon," Jax said, looking at her pointedly.

Jason straightened from his slightly stooped position. "You and the lady have nothing to discuss."

Megan took in the exchange. "Sure, Jackson. Give me a call."

She'd never talked with the younger Savage outside social situations such as this one, but she knew he wouldn't find it difficult to get her number.

Jax smiled. "Enjoy your burger. I put some bacon on it for you."

"Thanks."

She watched as he walked away, and then opened the bun and fished out the pork in question, putting it on the side of her plate closest to Jason. She wasn't surprised when he immediately snatched the strips up and ate them.

"Shall I ask what just happened?" she said.

Jason narrowed his eyes at her; they glinted dangerously in the dim light. "Ask all you want."

"Mmm. Just don't expect to get any answers: is that what you're saying?"

His grin was slow but ultimately complete. "I always knew there was a reason I liked you."

For a moment, one brief, irrefutable moment, Megan's gaze fused with his and a thrill of recognition swept through her—awareness, sexual, full and strong.

She caught her breath.

Jason appeared as puzzled as she did before finally breaking visual contact.

He reached for her fries again and she let him take a couple.

Her cell phone rang shrilly on the bar.

Dari!

She scooped up the phone and slid off the stool, heading toward the door.

"Hi, baby," she cooed, her heart expanding to fill her entire body....

2

THE FOLLOWING MORNING dawned earlier than it had the day before, or at least it seemed that way.

Megan dragged herself out of bed, went for her usual six-mile run, then showered and dressed for a day at the office rather than at the training facility. She had back-to-back meetings, so any thoughts of working her frustrations out on the firing range or on overly eager new recruits went out the window.

Last night, she'd barely spoken to Dari before the line went dead. After five minutes of trying to get him back, she'd received a text message: Sorry, baby. Situation went south, reception bad. Love you.

She'd finally fallen asleep somewhere around 4:00 a.m., the cell clutched to her chest. But he hadn't called or texted again.

Feeling marginally better now that she had immediate business to occupy her time, she sat down in her office chair and considered the paperwork on the desk in front of her. She had yet to decorate the room in any way and heard about it from the two secretaries who manned the front, along with the pretty receptionist Jason was trying to charm. Megan's immediate response was to ask why they weren't on any of the men to do something about the starkness of their offices.

But maybe she should buy a couple of plants or something. There was good light in this room. And the view of the mountains through the window was great. Not that she spent that much time looking at it.

The telephone buzzed, indicating an internal call rather than an external one. She picked up the receiver.

"You ready?" Jason asked.

"For what?"

"The meeting in ten."

"I could do this one with my eyes closed."

"Right. You do realize that a one-year contract that will employ ten, twenty agents hangs in the balance."

"Mmm. So I've been told. By you, as the case may be. Anyway, I figured you have it covered."

"No, Meg, I think this one's going to take a woman's touch."

Twenty minutes later, she saw what he meant. The two representatives from a chain of area nightclubs they were meeting with were women. And they not only appeared immune to Jason's charms, they looked a wink away from offended.

This was the type of contract Dari could have finalized with a handshake. Instead, Megan took the reins and convinced them that Lazarus was the firm for the job.

Finally, she and Jason were alone in the conference room.

"Good job," he said with a grin.

"You might consider working on your skills when it comes to female clients."

"Why? I have you for that."

She gathered her items together and started to leave the office.

"You sitting in on the next one?" Jason asked.

"Women again?"

His grin widened. "No, men. But I think you'd be equally effective...albeit in a different way."

"I think I'll pass."

She heard voices and the tinny sound of a television coming from the front. She put her papers on her desk and went to investigate, unsurprised to find Jason already there.

"What's going on?" she asked.

The three women were gathered around a flat-screen TV usually reserved for training videos. They parted like the Red Sea, allowing her a clear view of live news coverage.

"Missing girl," Jason said, crossing his arms.

In Florida.

A missing girl who was so sweet-looking the case had garnered national attention. She picked up the remote to check. Sure enough, another national news channel was playing the same footage.

She and Jason turned toward their offices at the same time.

"Do you want to call or should I?" Jason asked, passing her open doorway where she already had a telephone in hand.

"You work your contacts, I'll work mine." She shouted for one of the secretaries, requesting she get the other available partners on the job. "First one to the finish wins...."

3

CHALLENGE WAS JASON Savage's middle name and had been ever since he was an unwanted kid. Never one to wallow in the past, he rarely thought about an upbringing that would make anyone gasp...and he certainly never used it to elicit sympathy from the opposite sex. He could count on three fingers the number of people who knew what motivated him... and the first two only because they'd gone through it with him.

The third...well, he was in Afghanistan now.

Speaking of which...

Jason had no sooner pulled the rented SUV to a stop in front of the motel the Lazarus group would call home base in central Florida than Darius's girl hopped out of the passenger's seat, her polished combat boots hitting the ground running.

He shook his head, put the car in park and shut off the engine, leaving the keys in the ignition in case it was needed fast.

Jason stared after her, thinking of his friend. In the four months since Dari'd shipped off, he'd been impressed with Megan at every turn. Oh, sure, he knew she was a Marine, and that allowed for a measure of capability, but she surpassed his expectations. She was strong and smart and knew her way around a minefield.

He'd no sooner made his own contact regarding the missing kid than she'd popped up in his open doorway with one of her own. In his case, it was an old college buddy who'd gone into intelligence and was something or other in the FBI.

Hers was the local sheriff who appeared to be happy for any professional help.

Within four hours the team was on the ground, motel rooms and transportation arranged, and a game plan sketched out.

Jason suddenly realized that his gaze was glued to Megan's ass under the khaki of her pants. Damn, but the girl had a body on her.

He swallowed thickly and got out of the truck. While it wasn't the first time he'd appreciated her curves—sometimes even in front of Dari—for some reason, his attention seemed inappropriate now.

Megan turned toward him. "Jason Savage, this is Deputy Adams. He's going to be acting as liaison between us and the sheriff's office."

He shook the deputy's hand, friendly enough but instantly dismissing the kid. Jason knew he wasn't going to be any help at all. He'd be lucky to find his johnson in a windstorm.

"This the place?" he said unnecessarily, since he already knew it was. But it gave him an excuse to round the deputy. He was Megan's contact; she could handle him.

And if the way the deputy hiked up his pants in disdain at his obvious dismissal was any indication, Jason had the feeling she was going to have her work cut out for her.

Locals.

But it was important for the hazards team to have an in there. The sheriff and his personnel could cause them a lot of grief if they weren't playing on the same side.

He stepped up to the motel sidewalk and walked to the first room, pushing open the door. "Central command," he said. "Everybody stow their stuff and meet here in ten." He then walked over to the second room, where he planned to claim as his own quarters.

He wasn't surprised to see Megan choose the next room down, and the rest of the five-person team they'd brought with them following suit down the line.

He left his door open and dropped his duffel on the foot of the bed before going into the small bathroom in the back and washing his face. No matter where he was, the feel of cold water always gave him the sensation of being in control. It helped shrug off the dirt and hassles from travel and regroup for the task at hand.

And right now that happened to be finding little Finley Szymanski....

WITHIN TWENTY MINUTES a large swivel whiteboard had been brought in that boasted a corkboard on the other side, along with other organizational equipment. Megan walked in front of it, tacking photos of the missing seven-year-old to the board along with physical characteristics, while Jason pinned up a map, indicating where the girl had gone missing and the location of her house.

"According to the report, she was out bike riding at around seven the last anyone saw her," Jason said.

"Was the bike found?"

"No."

"Who saw her?"

"A neighbor."

"The last time she had contact with a family member?"

"Five-thirty, just after dinner. Her sister."

"How old is the sister?"

"Ten."

"Friends?"

Jason uncapped a marker and enlarged dots already made on the map. "These are where her friends live..."

The last one he circled edged a large thatch of forest.

They all leaned back and groaned.

"Right," Megan said. "We're talking over twenty-five hundred acres of land here. And I don't think I have to point out that this area of Florida has had a lot of rain and the ground is oversaturated. As a result, there are some parts the sheriff's personnel haven't been able to reach yet."

"Are you kidding me?" Dominic Falzone asked. "What, are they afraid of getting their feet wet?"

A couple of chuckles and added insults.

Megan looked toward the door where she knew the deputy was talking to the motel manager just outside.

"We'll be working together as a team, guys, so I'd appreciate it if you could keep the insults to a minimum."

Dominic Falzone was a decorated war vet, a tried-and-true Marine, but his mouth had landed the dark-haired, dark-eyed Lazarus team member into more than his fair share of hot water.

Jason stepped up. "Since conditions today are much like they were yesterday, search personnel probably guessed there was no way the girl could have gotten in and out of those areas by herself."

Megan's fingers tightened on her own marker.

Of course, what went unsaid was that someone could have taken her in there.

"Listen up, this is the plan…"

Within ten minutes Jason had outlined where he

wanted them to enter the forest, each at twenty-five-yard intervals.

"Okay, we don't have much usable daylight left," he said. "Grab your gear and let's get going."

It was only 4:00 p.m., but since it would be darker inside the forest without direct sunlight, they estimated maybe three hours before they'd have to call it quits for the night.

Of course, Megan fully expected there to be objections.

She hefted her own bag and followed the team out of the room, watching where Lazarus partner Lincoln Williams stood against the wall outside, having listened without participating, every bit the spook he had once been with the FBI, smoking a cigarette. He pitched it to the curb and followed.

IT WAS AFTER TEN before they returned to the motel and after midnight before the command center emptied out except for him and Megan. Other team members had returned to their own rooms to catch what sleep they could before rising again at 5:00 a.m.

Jason sat back in one of the extra chairs that had been brought in. While they were away, the motel owner had arranged to have the beds removed and chairs and two folded tables brought in instead. Jason didn't feel tired in the least. They'd made good ground today. But they needed to find the girl soon.

"Where did Linc get off to?" Megan asked, stretching.

"Lord knows. Even when he's here, I hardly know it."

A ghost of a smile. "Tell me about it. The guy's as big as a train car, but if he doesn't want to be seen, he won't be."

Jason thought about pushing the box of cold hot wings her way, wondering if she'd refuse. He hadn't seen her eat much of anything all day, always busy doing something or other, either checking notes or surveying the map and detailing tomorrow's route.

He nearly sighed in relief when she reached for the box herself, pulling it forward and taking out one of the sticky chicken wings. He leaned back and took a beer from a cooler, twisted off the top and handed it to her.

"Thanks."

He opened himself one and then rocked back on the chair legs, watching her.

She made no attempt to take dainty bites, the way he'd seen countless women before her do. And when she took a pull from the beer, it was a genuine tip-your-head-back slug that emptied half the bottle.

He grinned and absently rubbed his chin. If not for the way her T-shirt emphasized her breasts, he might think she was one of the guys.

His gaze homed in on her mouth and he felt a strangely familiar tightening of his pants across his groin. Oh, no, even without makeup and a dress, there was absolutely nothing masculine about Megan McGowan.

"What?"

He blinked up into her blue eyes, realizing he'd been caught. "Nothing." He pointed toward her mouth. "You've got a bit of sauce…yeah, right there."

She wiped at the red dot with her napkin and continued eating.

"Good?"

"Huh?" She looked at the wing in her hand. "I didn't even notice. I'm operating on automatic right now."

Jason let the chair legs clunk to the floor. "Yeah, me, too."

"They're not bad, I guess." She shrugged. "I'm not a big wings girl, really."

"What kind of girl are you, really?"

She smiled. "A regular fried-chicken kind of girl."

He chuckled and swallowed a good portion of his beer.

He wasn't sure what he'd expected her to say. Given the direction of his earlier thoughts, maybe something like filet mignon or salmon.

Instead, she'd chosen what might possibly be an even sloppier and more fattening alternative.

This from the girl who had passed on fries the other night.

Of course, like him, she understood her body needed the calories. Running as they had that day, they could easily burn double a regular day's nutrients.

"You're staring again." She laughed.

"I am?" He was.

Jason ran his hand over his face, watching as she checked her silent cell phone for the tenth time in the past ten minutes.

"Heard anything more?" he asked.

She shook her head. "You?"

"Nope. Figured you were lucky to have heard from him when you did. Lord only knows how long he'll be out."

He watched her frown.

In all the time Megan and Dari had been a couple, he didn't think he'd talked to her as much as he had in the past four months. Or looked at her more than he had today. She was his best friend's girl—period.

Yeah? Then what was he still doing there watching her eat rather than hightailing it back to his own room for some shut-eye?

"So…" he said. "You two talk about getting hitched?"

Her brows hiked up on her forehead. "Nah. Not seriously."

"But you have talked about it."

She shrugged noncommittally, her movements seeming to slow.

Finally, she put down the wing she was eating and wiped her hands.

"Well," she said, looking everywhere but at him. "It's going to be an early morning, so I think I'm going to hit the sack."

Jason cleared his throat. "Yeah, me too."

She began gathering the boxes and empty bottles on the table.

"Leave it. I'll make sure the motel staff picks it up before five."

"Thanks."

She moved toward the door. Was it his imagination, or did she seem a little distracted?

"God. Where is my head?"

She backtracked to the table and picked up her phone.

She'd forgotten her cell?

"Well...good night."

Jason cleared his throat and reached for another beer. "Good night."

He stopped short of adding "Sweet dreams." Truth was he was afraid his dreams tonight were going to be too sweet. And chances were high they were going to feature her....

4

MEGAN LAY BACK in the king-size motel room feeling as if sand coated her eyeballs. It was after two and she hadn't been able to close her eyelids for more than a moment, much less fall asleep. Which was par for the course lately.

She reached over to check her quiet cell and then lie back again with a heavy sigh.

In recent weeks, she'd become aware of a sort of silent humming. Oh, she missed Dari with her head and her heart. But her body had been fine. Of course, sexting had probably helped. But now, now she felt as if she wanted to jump out of her skin it was so uncomfortably alive.

The sensation began at the tip of her toes, traveled upward to her inner thighs, making her nipples constantly hard, making her panties constantly damp.

An image of Jason chanced through her mind. She frowned, attributing the aberration to the fact she'd just seen him.

She groaned and rolled over onto her side, back to the nightstand and the cell phone on top of it. Despite the nonstop hum of the air conditioner under the window, it was still hot and she wore nothing but a white tank top and a pair of white cotton panties. She'd stripped the blankets back and was lying on the sheets. But the humidity was brutal and seemed to contribute to her sense of longing.

Without realizing that's what she had in mind, she slipped her hand between her thighs so her wrist pressed against her damp crotch and then she squeezed her muscles together tightly. She groaned again as white-hot need shot through her every cell.

She'd been known to take matters into her own hands before. But certainly not since meeting Dari. He saw to every one of her needs and beyond.

But now that he was gone, she was all too aware she was a living, breathing female in need of release, preferably with a willing, skilled male.

Of course, her male was thousands of miles away in a sweltering desert just then, and her release was nowhere to be found.

She rolled back onto her back, shifting her hand so that it lay directly against her aching womanhood through the damp cotton. Heat shimmered up to her breasts and then sank back down to pool in her lower belly.

Yes…

It had been four long months since she'd felt

Dari…right there. Touching her. Thrusting deep into her…

She stroked herself through the cotton and restlessly licked her lips, surrendering to what she was about to do and ultimately embracing it. Only, the connection wasn't nearly intimate enough, so she edged her fingertips under the elastic of her panties, diving lower still until they met with her slick, shallow channel.

Megan stretched her head back and moaned, riding the delicious waves of sensation, a willing surfer bent on exploring deeper waters.

She ran her fingertips along the damp length of her swollen folds, working her middle into the tight pool for a dip. Her muscles immediately contracted, closing around the digit, begging for an even more meaningful meeting.

Her other hand trailed down her stomach until it, too, took up residence under the cotton of her panties. But where her left had focused on exploring dark, damp places, her right found her fleshy center, rubbing against it once, twice…

Megan gasped, her muscles contracting, allowing her the release she'd sought. She rode it out, welcoming every last spasm even as she clamped her legs together, trapping her hands where they were.

For long moments she lay there, absently stroking her pulsing flesh, curious as to why her cheeks were suddenly damp. She was surprised to find she was crying…

JASON SQUINTED UP at the blinding orange ball of the midday sun, thinking conditions couldn't possibly be worse.

"Things could always be worse," Megan said next to him. "There could be a hurricane heading this way."

He stared at her. "Is there?"

"Nah."

"Thank God for small favors."

He blew out a long breath from between his teeth, staring at the clearing around them. Five minutes ago they'd both emerged to find the nonstop rain they'd woken up to this morning was being replaced by the scorching sun. It didn't feel like a sauna—it felt worse.

Megan plucked the material of her T-shirt away from where it clung, soaked, to her stomach. He tried not to watch, but couldn't help himself.

Another team member emerged from across the fifty-yard clearing in the middle of the forest.

"Anything?" Megan called.

The agent indicated in the negative and then backed up until he was once again protected by the tree line.

Good idea.

Jason did the same and Megan followed suit. He glanced at his watch. They'd been at it since early this morning. That meant five hours of slogging through the trees with only a minimum of breaks, a protein bar and water bottle the only sustenance.

Megan leaned against the trunk of a tall pine and drank sparingly from her own canteen, dragging the back of her hand across her mouth afterward as she considered the clearing.

"Not a scrap of fabric, no sign of tracks…nothing."

Jason grimaced. "Same here."

Of course, had any of them found anything, they would have contacted the others via the radios they each carried.

Jason picked up his radio and told the rest of the team about the clearing, then advised they take at least a twenty-minute break and eat something before continuing.

Megan edged down slightly, propping her back against the tree in a semiseated position without actually sitting down. The ground was so sodden, she was denied that luxury.

"Christ, it's hot," she said.

"Tell me about it. I'd take a hundred and twenty degrees in the desert heat of Afghanistan over this any day."

She looked at him. "Me, too."

They fell silent. Jason quietly cursed himself. He hadn't meant to inspire thoughts of Dari, but he was sure that's where her mind had wandered. If he had any doubt, all he had to do was watch her take out her cell and check it before frowning and putting it back in her pocket.

They'd all been supplied with lunch rations,

modified MRE—meals ready-to-eat—that were fresher and a little more appetizing, but just as safe and portable. He took his out and offered it to Megan. She stared up at him.

"Thanks, but I have my own."

Her curious gaze made him look the other way, even as he tore open the package. Of course she had her own. What the hell was he thinking, offering her his?

He wasn't sure what was happening here, but he'd better snap out of it before Megan started thinking something was up.

Problem was, something *was* up. Big-time. Last night he'd woken up in the middle of the night with a massive hard-on…and it had Megan's name written all over it.

He was relieved when Dominic popped up some twenty yards to his right and headed in their direction.

"Hey," he said, leaning against a tree on the other side of Jason.

They answered in kind and all three ate in relative silence.

"There's still so much ground we're missing," Megan said quietly, tucking away the wrapper from a piece of cheddar.

Dominic said, "We could have organized the volunteers lined up outside the sheriff's office."

"In this weather? We would have ended up searching for half of them." Jason shook his head. "It was just as well the sheriff sent them to the mall and other public venues where they could keep an eye out but stay out of the elements."

"Besides," Megan added, "in cases like these, untrained individuals haven't a clue what they're looking for. Shortly into a search of this nature, they generally stop paying attention and are more at risk of accidentally trampling evidence than finding any."

"Which is why we're here."

Dominic took a deep breath. "We getting paid for this?"

Megan and Jason shared a look.

"You are," Megan said.

"And the company will if we deliver results."

Essentially that was the deal they'd struck with the sheriff's office. From what Jason understood, they had a matching guarantee from the federal government by way of Lincoln's FBI friend…all on the down low, of course.

Of course, that actually depended on whether or not they found the girl.

Megan pushed up off the tree and stashed her wrappers in her pockets.

"I'm heading back out. See you on the other side…"

5

Eight days and no results...

MEGAN STOOD AT the sink in her motel bathroom and stared at herself in the mirror, the light slanting through the doorway only slightly breaking the darkness. The cold water she'd doused her face with dripped down over her chin, spots dotting her black T-shirt. Over a week of grueling days spent scouring thick thatches of dark woods, hampered by rain and heat. A sensation of sheer exhaustion combined with growing fear that they may not find little Finley Szymanski created a dark cloud that pressed from within as well as without.

She listlessly reached for a coarse towel and patted her chin and throat dry. It didn't help that she had yet to hear from Dari. Every moment that ticked by inched up the worry quotient and made her itch in places she couldn't possibly scratch on her own.

Areas she tried to ignore, ones that transcended the mere physical.

She put the towel down and went back into the other room where the television droned on, broadcasting the late local news, which was dominated by the continuing search for the missing girl. The team's final briefing of the day had broken up a short while ago, each member returning to his room, all of them experiencing discouragement to some degree, but vowing that tomorrow was another day.

Megan sat down on the edge of the made bed and checked her cell where it lay on the nightstand before grabbing the remote and flicking through the stations.

"Don't bother. News and more news," Jason said from the open doorway.

Deciding she was tired of the endless rattle of the air conditioner, not to mention the soggy, barely cold air it coughed out, she'd asked the front office for a fan and more often than not, she also left the door open until it was time to sleep.

She tossed the remote to the bed. "You're right."

He pushed from the jamb and came inside. "I'm always right."

She smiled. "I'd laugh if I didn't think you believed that."

He sat down on the edge of the bed next to her, near but not touching. "Have I not proven myself and then some yet?"

Strangely, he had. But he was the last one she'd
let know that.

She fingered the cell phone again, tilting it to look
at the blank display.

When she turned back, she caught Jason watching
her, wearing an expression with which she'd become
familiar in recent days…and found somewhat dis-
concerting. If only because it touched some of those
itchy places.

"What?" she asked.

"Oh, nothing. Just thinking that it must be hard.
You know, to be in the middle of this and having Dari
so far away and out of contact."

She looked forward and nodded. "Yeah."

They sat silently for a few minutes.

The nightly visits had become a ritual of sorts, with
one or the other of them showing up at the other's
room for a few minutes of conversation, something to
help them relax a bit after official business was taken
care of. Megan realized she'd come to look forward
to them.

Maybe a little too much.

She slanted him a look. "You know, you don't have
to do this…"

"Do what?"

"Take care of me."

"Who says I'm doing this for you?"

She laughed. "Right. Isn't there a barmaid or waitress somewhere you should be chatting up?"

He rubbed his chin and averted his gaze, his self-conscious expression making her throat tighten in awareness.

Uh-oh…

JASON CONSIDERED HER QUESTION and what he'd almost said in response—that lately he wanted no one but her.

He ran his fingers through his hair several times and pushed from the bed. This wasn't happening. There was no way he was gunning for his best friend's girl.

Why, then, wasn't he with the waitress he'd met the other night? She'd slipped him her number with his beer and she'd certainly been a stunner. Just his type with golden-blond hair, lush curves and a smile designed to make any guy think of getting her between the sheets.

But whenever he imagined taking a woman to bed, the only woman he was thinking about was Megan.

Which was crazy. He wasn't *that* guy. The one who slept with his best friend's girl.

He turned around and bumped straight into her, not realizing she'd also gotten up and stood behind him.

She was close. Too close. Their noses were nearly touching.

The first thing he registered was the clean scent of her skin. Just the soft smell of motel soap, no perfume, no flowery lotion.

The next thing he saw was the way she licked her lips anxiously.

Jason groaned deep in his throat.

This…was…not…happening…

"Um, I think I better go," he managed to grind out, trying not to notice the way the hard tips of her breasts strained against her tank top, skimming the wall of his chest with every shallow breath she took.

"Yeah. That, would, um, be a good idea."

Neither one of them moved.

Truth was, Jason was afraid to. He was afraid that if he twitched a muscle, it would be to back her up against that bed and down on top of it.

No, she would have to be the one to move first.

Hopefully away from him.

Instead, she stepped in closer.

Christ…

MEGAN CAUGHT HER BREATH. To say she hadn't known this might happen would make her a liar. She and Jason had been working too closely together over the past ten days for some attraction not to develop.

They probably should have been a little more careful, though.

Of course, she had no way of knowing her power to deny her own fundamental needs would hover somewhere around zero when the moment did occur.

Or accept the possibility that Jason's would, too…

She swallowed hard, watching his eyes sharpen, much like a black panther that had just caught sight of his mate. His nostrils flared slightly as he tried to drag in air that suddenly seemed scarce in the too-hot room. She could smell his sweat…and, yes, his sex.

She was caught between needing to step away, yet yearning to move closer.

Without realizing that's what she was going to do, she leaned ever so slightly forward, pressing her open mouth against his in the lightest of kisses. She didn't expect him to respond. But the instant their lips made contact, she felt a fire ignite in her veins, burning her from the inside out. She wanted him to respond.

Oh, God…

He groaned somewhere deep in his chest and she felt his hands on her upper arms, as if poised to push her away. Instead, he hauled her closer.

Megan caught her breath, unprepared to have him crush his mouth down on hers…or for her welcome of the thought-robbing action.

Urgency welled up in her stomach and then exploded outward as she tangled her tongue with his. It had been so very long, too long since she'd felt this depth of need for a man.

Then it dawned on her how long—four months.

She broke free from him, gasping for air and pressing the back of her hand against her mouth.

"I'm…sorry," she rasped.

Jason stepped back. "I'm the one who should

be apologizing. I… We… That should never have happened."

"I know."

They turned away from each other, Megan trying like hell to grasp the situation.

What was she thinking? She loved Dari. Missed him. Lived for his texts and phone calls.

So what, then, was she doing practically devouring Jason?

It didn't make any sense.

And yet it made perfect sense.

"You know, what just happened had nothing to do with either of us," Jason said.

Megan's heart skipped a beat at his words.

She slowly turned back to face him.

"Look, what I'm about to say probably won't excuse my behavior. But maybe it will help explain it."

She nodded. "Go ahead."

"Well, the best I can figure it, what just happened doesn't mean there's really anything between them."

"Then what does it mean?"

"Physical need—plain and simple."

She bit her bottom lip, trying, but failing, to quiet the pool of desire in her lower stomach.

"But the kiss…"

She stared at him.

"The kiss was too intimate."

She released a breath. "Oh, boy, you're not lying there."

The side of his mouth inched up in a smile. "So let's not kiss."

"Pardon me?"

He slowly lifted his hand and ran his fingers through his shortly cropped brown hair. The simple gesture emerged both hot and appealing.

"I'm saying, let's not kiss."

"Good idea…"

She began to walk toward the bathroom.

He caught her arm, his grip soft but insistent.

"Let's just sleep together…"

6

JASON WATCHED MEGAN'S face closely, identifying each emotion as it passed. Shock, disbelief, then ultimately intrigue.

He prided himself on being a man who called 'em as he saw 'em. And now that he understood that his physical need for Megan was returned, well, there was no reason for them to pretend it wasn't.

"Jason, I..."

He could sense her withdrawing. "What, Megan? We're both adults. Marines, even. We know the difference between real emotion and physical need. Just like a wound that requires attention, there are other... needs that have to be met."

Her blue eyes sparkled. "Yes, but unlike a wound, this can go without treatment."

He grinned. "Can it?"

She faltered.

"Look, I know the kiss bothered you. Hell, it bothered me, too." He grimaced, thinking her mouth had felt all too good pressed against his. "I'm not that guy. You know, the one that screws around with his best friend's girl."

"Funny, when I first met you, that's exactly what I figured you for."

He squinted at her. "And now?"

She looked down. "And now that I know you better, I think you're just as caught off guard by this as I am."

That was a good sign, no?

"So," she said, "if this is not that, then what is it?"

"Sex. Pure and simple."

The dubious expression returned.

"Look. We don't have to kiss," he said. "Actually, I'd prefer it if we didn't."

"And how do you propose we…have sex without it?"

He couldn't help grinning in purely carnal desire. "Simple—you turn around…"

THE MERE IDEA SENT decadent shivers racing over her skin. She rubbed her arm and his gaze followed the movements, catching not only the goose bumps there but the way her nipples hardened beneath the cotton of her T-shirt.

"No one needs to know," he said quietly. "Just you and me. And it will only be once."

Unless…

The unsaid word hung there.

"The way I see it, you're not betraying Dari. If anything, by having sex with me, you're staying true to him."

That made her laugh.

"Think about it. If it were anyone else but me, well, there might be a real threat there."

His words made a twisted kind of sense.

She felt his hands on her hips.

"What are you doing?"

"Let's just see if this has possibilities…"

She resisted the urge to let him turn her around at first, then gave in, her heart thudding thickly in her chest. She heard the door close and the room went dark as he shut off the light and switched on the air conditioner.

She began to turn around to put a stop to this insanity, when she felt his hard arousal pressed against her backside.

She moaned.

God, oh God, but that felt so good…

His fingers tightened on her hips, holding her still.

She heard the click of her swallow.

"I think…" she rasped, licking her lips restlessly.

She fell silent, wondering at the pure need swirling through her and pooling in a deep, dark pool in her womb.

"You think?"

His breath against her ear made her shiver.

"I think this, um, could work…"

That's all the impetus either of them needed. He tugged at the bottom of her T-shirt at the same time she did.

"Take care of yours, I'll take care of mine," she told him. "No seduction scene necessary…"

Keeping her back turned, she quickly stripped out of her clothes, overly aware he was doing the same behind her. She made out the sound of a foil packet being ripped open, smelled the latex and readied herself for…

Oh!

He slid his long, thick length between her thighs without preamble. Megan squared her legs and then bent over, bracing her hands against the bed. She began to reach back, but he was already guiding his impressive shaft to slide between her swollen folds, finding her slick and waiting.

Oh, yes…

It seemed so very long since she'd known the intimacy of sex. And with him behind her, out of her line of sight, it was easy to forget who he was…and imagine him as Dari instead.

Her throat tightened.

Okay, maybe not Dari. Even in this position, he would find a way to kiss her.

No. Maybe she'd imagine this was a dream. Not unlike what she accomplished during her own solo sessions when she brought herself to climax.

This was just that. A desperate seeking of physical release.

He pressed his hand against her lower back, holding her still as he positioned himself against her tight, damp sex…and then breached it, chasing both the air from her lungs, and all thought from her head.

Oh, sweet Jesus, yes…

Jason slowly slid in to the hilt, stilling. She shifted on her feet slightly, finding a more satisfying spot, bunching her hands in the bedspread as she bore back against him, taking him deeper yet.

Then he finally moved, withdrawing, creating sensations even sweeter than before. Until he thrust… then thrust again, grasping her hips to hold her still as he showed her just all she'd been missing, what she'd been craving, and what he could give her now…

Her hands slid on the bedspread and she pitched forward, completely willing to climb on top of the bed and continue there.

But Jason appeared to have another thought in mind.

Withdrawing completely, he backed up, his hands guiding her. He sat down on the desk chair. Megan gladly spread her knees and sat down, reaching between her thighs to guide his hard length back where she wanted to feel it most.

She slid down slowly, the new position offering a different sensation. She gasped when he was in to the hilt then braced her hands against his knees and leaned forward, rocking her hips forward, then back...

With the baton firmly in her hand, she took great pleasure in setting the languid pace, reveling in every shimmer of her muscles, every tingle in her womb. She swore she could hear Jason gritting his teeth behind her, which ramped up her own excitement as she considered the view he had of her.

He mumbled something under his breath and then grasped her hips tightly, holding her still. Megan braced her feet on the lower chair rungs and moved her hands to her own knees, barely stable before he thrust his hips upward, filling her...

Megan moved her hips, more of an involuntary jerking, the breath leaving her body as Jason continued to slam upward into her convulsing flesh. Her lungs froze, her stomach seized and the release she'd been working toward exploded, sending shock waves through her body. She grasped her own knees more tightly, his long, hard thrusts drawing out the overpowering sensations even as his rapid breathing told of his own impending climax.

She heard a long, winding groan and knew he'd found it.

Nothing but the sound of the air conditioner and their heavy breathing filled the room as she leaned back against him. His hands skimmed her inner thighs, lingering briefly on her damp, quivering flesh, and then budged up over her trembling stomach before finally cupping her breasts.

A fresh thrill ran the length of her.

They were both tired and sweaty.

"More?" he whispered into her ear.

Megan swallowed hard. "Oh, God, yes…"

TWO HOURS LATER, Megan had collapsed facedown on the bed, Jason dropping on top of her. Finally, she felt adequately satisfied. At one point, he'd complained that he wasn't enough man for her and she'd laughed…before bringing him to full erectness again and riding him for all he was worth.

"What time is it?" Jason asked.

The bedspread was half over the nightstand, blocking the clock. Megan yanked on it twice before it slid off.

"After two."

"I need to hightail it back to my room. We've got to be up in three hours."

She hummed her agreement but noticed neither one of them made any effort to move.

She wiggled her bottom slightly.

Finally, he groaned and rolled off her.

"Woman, you're insatiable."

She stayed where she was, her head turned the other way. "I don't recall hearing any complaints." She smiled against the sheets. "Oh, okay. Maybe one."

"That wasn't a complaint. It was a statement of wonder."

She laughed huskily. "Mmm…"

He slapped her bare ass. It stung but she was too relaxed to make any kind of clear response beyond whispering, "Ow."

"I'm going. You'll want to lock the door behind me."

"It self-locks."

"Not the chain."

"Someone would have to be insane to try to break in here."

"Yeah, well, there are a lot of crazies running around out there."

"Fair enough."

She didn't budge.

"Megan."

"What?"

"Come lock the door."

"I will." She waved at him.

He chuckled and then left the room, closing the door quietly behind him.

Megan nestled into the bed more comfortably and promptly dropped off to sleep, thankful to have a friend like Jason....

7

THE FOLLOWING MORNING, Megan felt as if she'd run a fifty-mile marathon—and won. Gone was the stress that had weighed heavily on her like a constant load and she was able to refocus her energies on the job at hand.

If she felt a secret little thrill every time she and Jason passed each other within smelling distance, well, only the two of them had to know that.

No, she didn't want him again. In fact, she hadn't really had him. Not in any way that counted. They'd been two adults seeking physical release and had found it.

She took a deep breath, feeling more relaxed than she had in months, and was thankful.

It was 7:00 a.m. and the half of the team dedicated to going back over the ground they'd already covered had already left. Now the remaining members—including her and Jason—were discussing alternative approaches.

While their primary job was to conduct a physical search for Finley Szymanski, she suggested they broaden the scope to include investigative angles, the aim being to assist in the physical search. The more people they talked to, the better handle they'd have on where to look for the little girl.

Megan caught herself up short from adding, *The little girl's body.*

The more time that passed, the less likely they were to find the child alive. Statistics bore that fact out. It had been that reality that had weighed down on her day after day.

"So are we clear on what each of us is going to do?" she asked, checking the board where the assignments were outlined.

Jason would be holding down home base, while she'd go to the family's church to speak to friends of the Szymanski family. She'd tried on a couple of occasions for direct family access, but the sheriff's office had drawn the line at that, especially in light of recent events. After all, it only stood to reason that as frustrations rose, finger-pointing would start. The family was now under the glare of suspicion, making them even more difficult to get close to than when they were looked upon strictly as the poor, worried victims of a random crime.

Her phone vibrated where it was strapped to her belt.

Dari.

And it was a phone call rather than a text.

She knew a moment of hesitation.

What was she doing? She hurried to answer. "Hello?"

Too late. The call was redirected to voice mail.

Damn!

Her gaze was drawn to Jason where he spoke with a team member.

She tried for a smile and then walked out of the room, checking her cell again. When it indicated a voice mail had been received, she quickly retrieved it.

"I didn't want to tell you this way, but the plane's about to take off and this is my last shot. I'm coming home…"

Megan's heart dipped low and then boomeranged up.

He's coming home!

She looked over her shoulder at where Jason was checking his own cell phone.

He's coming home….

See you in a few hours, bro!

The simple message from Darius froze Jason in his tracks when he read the text on his cell phone. He lost his line of concentration and completely forgot about the team member he was talking to.

His gaze immediately sought out Megan as she was coming back inside the room. She looked as dazed as he felt.

"You don't like it?" Jonathon asked.

"Huh?" Jason pulled his attention back to the conversation at hand even as he slid his cell back into his pocket. Jonathon Reece was an ex-army grunt who looked all of fifteen with his surfer-dude looks. He was one of the newest Lazarus hires and had been brought on board because of his firsthand knowledge of the area. "No, no, it's fine. Run with it." He patted the kid on the shoulder and maneuvered him toward the door. "Check in later and report the results."

Thankfully Jonathon didn't linger any longer and exited the room. Which left him and Megan alone.

"He's coming home."

He knew he didn't have to be more specific. Dari would have contacted Megan before Jason. And even if he hadn't, he could tell by her expression that she knew.

"He's boarding a transport now."

Jason nodded, watching her face closely. He wouldn't have thought her the type to wallow in guilt. But he saw traces of it there. And he felt it himself. Of course, he understood they would be inhuman if they didn't experience something akin to the dark emotion. Neither of them had counted on Dari's returning so quickly. In fact, had the word come in twelve hours ago, last night would have never happened.

He never would have suggested what he had.

And he knew for certain Megan would never have accepted.

"Look," he said quietly. "I've been knocked back

on my heels along with you. But nothing's changed. There's no reason he ever has to find out."

He couldn't even bring himself to use his friend's name in the context of the conversation.

He'd never lied to Darius. And he reasoned he wouldn't really be lying to him now. The last thing Dari would ask him was if he'd banged his girl. Which meant that he'd never have to answer the question.

Megan nodded and pushed the wisps of hair that had escaped her ponytail back from her sexy face. "Right."

"You're happy?" he asked.

She squinted at him.

"At his coming back," he clarified.

He couldn't bear it if his indiscretion had turned Dari's girl away from him.

"Of course," she said.

She looked away from him, and Jason could tell by the wistful shadow in her eyes that she was, indeed, happy.

He released the breath he was holding. Good.

If there was a small part of him that wanted her to say otherwise, he wasn't going to acknowledge it. They'd had sex. Nothing more. Nothing less.

Mind-blowing, hot, sweaty, naughty sex…but sex nonetheless.

There was no love between them.

Not the love that so obviously existed between Megan and Dari.

Why, then, did he suddenly envy that love?

"I, um, am meeting Dominic in the car outside. We're going to ride over to the church," she said.

He knew that. After all, he'd just helped her map out the morning's activities just a few moments ago.

But within that time span, it seemed the whole world had tilted on its axis.

It was up to him to figure out a way to set it right.

Even if that meant doing nothing at all.

AN HOUR LATER, Megan looked around the simple house that sat next to the small chapel, the setup similar to countless others she'd seen in her lifetime, as well as attended in every town in which her father had been transferred to, growing up. There were faded, frilly curtains at the kitchen window, worn linoleum on the countertops and floors. A plate of homemade cookies on the table.

The current pastor had been in residence for the past year and a half and was maybe about thirty-five, forty, tops. He and his wife had two 'tween girls who were rushing adulthood, much like every other normal girl their age. He'd been happy to talk to her, to do anything he could to aid in the search for little Finley, but he hadn't given her much more than she already had.

Dominic waited outside, as she'd requested.

The rain had stopped and a blazing sun turned the atmosphere into a hazy sauna.

"I'm sorry, I'm afraid I didn't give you anything you could use, did I?" Pastor Dewayne Dryer said as he walked outside with her.

"I appreciate your time. I'm sure you've already talked to several people about the case."

He nodded. "And I'll talk to several others if it helps bring Finley home."

Megan noticed a couple of people walking into the chapel.

She gave the pastor a card that bore the main office's number along with the one to her cell, and asked him to add it to the pile he already had for those wanting a call if he thought of anything else.

She nodded toward the chapel. "Do you mind if I have a look around?"

His brows rose slightly. "No. No, of course not. Be my guest."

She slid her pad into her back pocket, and thanked him.

Dominic pushed from where he leaned against the SUV. She gestured for him to stay where he was as she walked the twenty yards or so to the chapel door.

Megan paused momentarily to allow her sight to adjust to the dimmer interior. Minimalism was the name of the game when it came to decorating. There were maybe twenty-five pews on either side of the aisle and a simple cross hung on the back wall. The pulpit was covered with blue indoor-outdoor carpeting, a plain podium to the left, what looked like a railing for the choir to the right. It smelled like cheap furniture polish and flowers, although she didn't see any fresh blooms. Had there been a recent funeral, maybe? Or a wedding.

She knew there had been several calls for prayer scheduled over the past ten days specifically geared toward the safe return of Finley. She counted sixteen people there now, spread around the pews. Most were elderly women, but there were two younger ones linked at the elbows to her left, and a man she guessed to be in his thirties to the right.

She edged toward the younger women, flashed her ID, which was nothing more than a private security badge and photo identification, although she was completely aware that it made her appear to be official law enforcement. She asked if she could speak to them and they quietly agreed, following her outside.

As it turned out, neither of them knew the girl. In fact, they didn't even live in the area. They'd come specially to put in a prayer for her from southern Georgia and planned on driving home straight after.

No, they hadn't talked to anyone else since their arrival a half hour ago.

No, they didn't know anyone else within driving distance.

Megan stifled her sigh and thanked them for their

time, about to call it quits when the man she'd spotted inside exited the chapel.

"Sir," she called. "Can I talk to you for a minute, please?"

She flashed her ID again. He looked beyond her to where Dominic still stood waiting at the SUV, his arms crossed over his impressive chest.

The man flashed her a smile. "Is there something I can help you with, Officer?"

She found out his name was Don McCain and that he sometimes played the organ at Sunday service if the regular organist was ill or on vacation. He was an elementary-school teacher, currently unemployed and, yes, he said, he knew the Szymanski family through the church.

"And little Finley? Had you ever interacted with her directly?"

"You mean, have I?"

She squinted at him in the hazy light.

"Present tense. You see, so many seem to have given up hope. I prefer to stay positive."

"I meant 'had' as in prior to this point," she said.

"Oh. I see." He slid his hands into his pants pockets, looking as if he'd just come from teaching a class of third graders with his starched white shirt, striped tie and beige slacks. He had light brown hair and eyes and an ordinary face with no distinguishing features.

"So…had you?"

He looked at her blankly. "Oh! Had I interacted

with Finley directly." He rocked back on his heels.
"Yes. In fact, I had. And I hope to again in the future.
She's such a bright little thing. And she likes looking
like a girl. Always wears this pretty pink scarf…"

Megan took notes even as her cell phone buzzed
on her hip.

He went on to say that he organized the seasonal
cookie sale to help benefit the church and that Finley
was one of their top sellers that year. With, of course,
plenty of help from her grandparents.

"And her mother?"

"Sorry to say I've never actually met her. I understand she doesn't get to church much."

Megan nodded as her phone buzzed again.

"Well, thank you for your time, Mr. McCain." She
produced her card and held it out. "Please add this
to the pile I'm sure you already have and add me to
the list of those wanting a call should you remember
anything else."

He held the card up. "You're actually the only one
I've talked to."

"Well, thank you, then."

She turned, sliding her cell from her holder at the
same time. Two missed calls. Neither one of them
from Dari. Or from Jason.

She sighed and put her phone back before heading
for the car.

"Where to next, boss?" Dominic said, opening
the passenger door for her.

"The first of three babysitters'."

8

LATER THAT AFTERNOON, Megan sat alone at the command center going over her notes. She'd been so distracted throughout the day, she hadn't given a lot of thought to the conversations she'd had or tried to take the precious little additional information she had received to the next level. Even her notes registered as chicken scratches in desperate need of an interpreter.

Unfortunately she didn't know of any hens around up for the job.

Cocks, on the other hand...

Her throat tightened and she closed her eyes.

She'd managed to meet up with only one of the three babysitters, and the girl had been as much help as rain on picnic day. Which was understandable, because just as she and the team were investigating different angles, so too were the sheriff's office and the FBI—which meant they were circling back to those with whom they'd already spoken and probing further. From what she could gather from this particular babysitter, they'd pushed her until she'd pushed them out.

Megan's patience with the girl had yielded her a few extra minutes, during which she'd gotten a couple of other park locations she'd once taken Finley that weren't already on the sheriff's or Lazarus's list.

Still, a check of the map showed them outside bike range for an adult, much less a seven-year-old girl.

"Don't move…"

Her pulse leaped at the familiar voice even as she felt hands lightly touch her shoulders, moving down over her arms and then back up again, pulling her with them.

Dari…

She turned and melted into his embrace, both glad to have him back—and relieved that she felt that way.

She stayed like that for a long moment, not moving, merely reveling in the feel of him against her again, sensing the thrum of his heartbeat, breathing in the soapy scent of his skin.

She released a breath she feared she'd been holding for over four months.

"Hey, you okay?" he whispered into her ear, smoothing her hair back.

She leaned back to gaze into his all-too-handsome face, but found her throat wouldn't allow her words. So she nodded instead.

"Wow," he said, grinning at her. "You did miss me, didn't you?"

You have no idea how much, she said silently.

She accepted his leisurely kiss, groaning at the welcome pressure of his mouth against hers. She shifted her feet for a closer meeting…and her knee hit something unexpected and hard.

She broke the kiss and looked down, finding a cast on the bottom half of his leg.

"What happened?"

His chuckle soothed her jangled nerves, but only slightly. "What, you didn't think they'd just let me come back on leave, did you?"

She'd been so overwhelmed she hadn't even stopped to think of why he was coming back. Only that he was.

"What happened? I mean, is it serious? Did you take a direct shot?"

A third voice sounded from the doorway. "Dumb-ass stepped on an IED."

Improvised explosive devise. They peppered any area where enemy combatants were rumored to be. Megan herself had watched two of her fellow Marines lose limbs to the crude weapons. Another lost his life.

"I didn't step on one," Dari said, his frown bone deep. "The interpreter traveling with us did. I was right behind him."

She didn't ask what happened to the interpreter as she searched his face.

"Metal where my femur used to be and significant muscle loss," he explained. "Trust me, it don't look pretty."

"But you have full use of your leg?"

He grinned. "I have full use of my leg."

Jason dropped the duffel he was hauling next to them. "Good. That means you can take care of your own business from here on in."

Megan averted her gaze, not wanting to read anything into his words, but failing.

Was she as much Dari's business as his duffel?

"I'm starved," Dari said, looking her over. "What's there to eat around here?"

She got the distinct impression he wasn't talking about food.

Jason cleared his throat. "Are we done?"

Dari looked over his shoulder. "Thanks for picking me up, Savage."

"I'll take that as a yes." He grimaced and gave his friend a two-finger salute. "I'll leave you two alone so you can catch up."

Megan held her breath until they were, indeed, alone. Then she released it.

"About that food…" Dari reminded her.

"Let's go back to my room," she said, hooking her finger into the waist of his khakis. "I'm sure I can find somebody who'll deliver…"

DARI LAID BACK IN BED, taking some comfort in having Megan's body curved against him while she slept, but not much. His leg was throbbing and his head wasn't doing much better. He'd been home for a little over six hours. Although he recognized that "home" was a relative term, because he was in Florida, not Colorado Springs.

Still, it was worlds away from the desolate, remote mountains of Waziristan, and much closer to home than he'd been two days ago.

If only he didn't find himself back there every time he blinked.

He absently rubbed the grit from his eyes. At least a week had passed since he'd gotten more than a couple hours of sleep at a stretch. Every time he closed his eyes, he found himself walking on that remote mountain pass, his M-16 gripped tightly in his hands, sweat running down the back of his camouflage shirt. The temps ranged somewhere near a hundred and ten degrees in the shade. Not that there had been much shade to be had where they were traveling. Which made it doubly important to keep aware of every step.

Only that was hard to do when your body was screaming and there didn't seem to be enough water in the world to quench your thirst. It had been two days since they'd stumbled across anything that remotely looked like civilized society. As you listened to the heavy breathing of those around you, as well as your own, it was all too easy to believe you were alone in the world. That nothing else existed.

Except for Megan…

He turned his head and watched her face as she slept. So beautiful.

Thoughts of her had kept him alive but hadn't staved off the memory of the interpreter half turning just ahead of him to let everyone know that they were still five klicks away from their first stopping point, when the sun glinted off something at his feet.

Darius had shouted for him to watch out. But it was too late. His foot landed and the IED exploded...

Now he ran his hand over his face, realizing it was drenched in sweat. Although for a moment, he remembered being drenched in something else entirely.

Megan shifted against him.

"Are you okay?" she whispered, her hand shifting to lie on his chest.

"Me? Sure. What makes you ask?"

"You made a strange sound."

"I did?"

Great.

He'd heard about flashbacks and had met with a psychologist in Germany where he'd been sent for the medical attention he required following the explosion. He'd been given a set of signs to look for indicating post-traumatic stress disorder.

Of course, he'd denied displaying any of the signs for fear that they'd keep him there longer.

At that point, all he could think about was making it back home.

Seeing Megan.

"I must have been dreaming," he said.

"Funny, I didn't think you were asleep."

He smiled at her in the dark. "Funny, I thought you were."

A twinge of pain in his leg made him wince. He considered getting the pain pills out of his bag and throwing back a couple, but decided against it. He was all too aware of how quickly someone could become addicted to those, as well, and wasn't about to go down that road.

"You hurt?"

"A little. Nothing I can't handle."

The dim neon light that filtered from the bathroom window bathed her in a red glow, highlighting the sweep of her dark hair, the pointy tips of her breasts, the curve of her hip.

He swallowed hard, wanting her all over again, no matter the price he would pay when he was done.

"Do you want a couple of ibuprofen?"

Funny, he hadn't thought of taking something a little less addictive. "That's a good idea."

He began to get up. She stayed him with a hand against his chest. "I'll get them."

He enjoyed watching her walk to the bathroom, her bare ass tight and perfect and her front just as enticing when she returned.

She handed him the two pills and a glass of water.

"Thanks."

"Sure."

She rounded the bed and climbed back into the other side, curving against him again. He put the glass down on the nightstand and then rested his chin on the top of her head.

"Having trouble sleeping?" she asked.

"Nah."

She tilted her face to look at him.

"Okay, maybe a little. It's been a long couple of days."

"I bet. When's the last time you got a good eight hours, uninterrupted?"

He recognized the question. It was one Marines asked other Marines when their capabilities were in doubt.

Of course, he and Megan weren't on patrol, but in a Florida motel room.

Still, he was hesitant to tell her. So rather than answering directly, he said, "I'm sure I'll be fine. I just need a little time to let my head catch up to my body."

Since no one's life was in his hands, he didn't think the white lie was that big a deal. While he'd like nothing better than to go out in a few hours and find that little girl, the search couldn't be in better hands than Megan and Jason's.

Speaking of which…

"So how have things been working out between you and Savage since I've been gone?" he asked.

She didn't answer for a long moment and the fingers she moved across his chest stilled.

"That bad, huh?"

"What?" She blinked.

"You and Savage."

"Oh. No. Actually, we've gotten along better than I would have ever thought."

He waited for her to continue. She didn't.

"I figured you guys would have been butting heads within five minutes."

"Me, too."

Her hand dipped a little lower on his abdomen. The air hissed between his teeth.

She smiled. "Now, my question is—do you really want to talk about business? Or shall we, um, continue catching up on pleasure?"

He grinned at her. "I don't know. Why don't you help me decide."

She curved her fingers around him, causing his semi-erect cock to instantly go fully rigid. She moved her hand slowly up, then down again, rubbing the pad of her thumb over the head.

Dari clenched his back teeth together, need for this one woman overwhelming every other thought in his head and pain in his body.

She leaned up and kissed him.

"Enough persuasion?" She squeezed him. "Or do you need more?"

"Depends."

She raised a brow. "Oh? On what?"

"On what else you're offering…"

He made out her half smile in the dim light. Then

she ran her tongue along the width of his chest, trailing a path down to where he already wanted her more than a man should want any woman.

At the warm, wet feel of her mouth on him, he let out a low groan, wishing the moment could last forever....

9

LATER THAT MORNING, Megan poured herself a cup of coffee in the command center. She was tired and anxious and really needed to gather her wits about her.

Dari was home.

For all intents and purposes, she was glad. Especially in light of the injuries he'd suffered.

Her heart contracted. To think how close she'd come to losing him…

She remembered his innocent question earlier about how she and Jason had gotten along while he was gone, then her hesitant response and ultimately her distracting techniques. It was uncomfortably ironic that she might still lose him.

Guilt. Pure, unadulterated guilt flowed through her.

The instant she identified the emotion, she was able to take a deep breath and release it.

Since receiving Dari's phone message the day

before, she'd been operating in a state of shock, trying to keep busy so she didn't have time to think
about what she had done. Then, all at once, he was
home and she'd gone into reactionary mode, playing
off him...playing with him.

But at some point in the morning hours, when
the lights were dim, and the immediacy of the situation relaxed, the tarlike substance coating her insides
thickened and she'd been forced to confront what lay
at the heart of her emotions: guilt.

"Let him see that expression and he's sure to know
something's up."

Jason's quiet presence at her elbow didn't surprise
her. His words did.

She tried to shake off her uneasiness and offered
up a wry smile. "Tell me about it."

She felt his gaze on her as she finished stirring
sugar and cream into her coffee.

"Hey," he said, touching her elbow. "Are you
okay?"

"I think 'okay' falls a little short of the mark."

She walked to the table, sipping her coffee while
she leafed through her notes.

"Anything I can do to help?"

She swallowed hard, trying not to look at him but
doing so anyway. "Isn't that the question that got me
into trouble in the first place?"

Pain flittered across his face, making her instantly
regret her terse response.

"Hey, you're not the only one in deep here," he said. "He is my best friend."

"And I'm his girl."

Silence fell and remained as they both considered the consequences of their hasty, ill-thought-out actions.

Megan wasn't used to this. She'd never had cause to feel guilty before. Not because she'd never done anything wrong, but because she'd always had a good reason for what she did.

Being in need of a good orgasm somehow wasn't rating high as far as good reasons went.

"Let me ask you a question," Jason said, coming to lean against the table next to her. "Would you feel as guilty if he wasn't back here on injury leave?"

"What?"

He didn't say anything for a long moment and then finally shrugged. "Hear me out. I think we're both wading through the same dark pool right now. One of my theories is that we feel even worse because while we were...well, you know, Dari's ass was on the line."

"He was injured ten days ago." She could have gone the rest of her life without looking at circumstances in that light.

"Same difference."

She reluctantly agreed. On more than the one count.

She focused on the papers without really seeing them. "I get your point."

"My advice?"

She looked at him.

"Let it go."

Easier said than done.

Just yesterday morning she would have thought otherwise. She *had* thought otherwise.

But now...

Jason cleared his throat. "Let's both focus on the job, get through the days. I'm guessing before you know it, things will return to normal."

Her coffee tasted bitter. She had the feeling it would have no matter how much sugar and cream she added. "My greatest fear is that 'normal' has been forever redefined."

"Only if you let it be."

She considered him from the corner of her eye. "Sounds like you're speaking from experience."

He gave her a long look.

"Right. Yes. Of course you are, aren't you?"

"What you need to remember is it didn't mean anything."

She bit on her bottom lip.

That was the problem. It didn't mean anything. Which made it all the more upsetting that she'd actually *done* it.

"Did it?" Jason asked quietly. "Mean anything?"

"No," she said a little too quickly. She took a deep breath. "No. It didn't mean anything to either of us. But, well, it will mean something to Dari."

There was a sound outside the room. They both

looked toward the open door where team members would be appearing any moment. It didn't surprise Megan to find Lincoln Williams peering inside, his mirrored glasses perched on his nose, his face expressionless.

Did the guy never sleep?

His head disappeared again.

"I have a feeling we're not the only ones who know what happened the other night," she said quietly.

"Linc? No worries there. It's hard enough to get him to speak, as it is. He won't be offering up anything."

She looked at him. "It's not him I'm worried about."

It was herself….

DARI KNOCKED BACK a slug of coffee and winced when one of the team members hit the foot of his injured leg as she passed by on her way to her chair in the command center.

"Sorry," she said quietly.

"No problem."

He only wished that were the case. The pain was even more intense now than it had been a few hours ago. Hell, a few days ago. He reasoned it was because of his grueling trip back home, a type of physical jet lag. It would help if he could trust himself to take the pain medication. But things weren't quite that bad… yet.

More sleep, however, might have helped.

But when he and Megan returned to her room, the last thing on his mind had been sleep.

He'd gone more than four long months without losing himself in the smell of her…the feel of her. And despite his pain, he'd intended to experience both as much as was physically possible.

Oh, and how he had. Just thinking about her soft moans and incredible body made him instantly hard.

He'd missed her more than he'd missed any one person ever. His thoughts had been on her far more than he would have believed possible, if only because he prided himself on keeping his mind on the job, not somewhere up in the clouds.

But every time he'd blinked, it had been her face he saw. Her smile he wanted to see. Her voice he wanted to hear. To the exclusion of almost all else.

Still, somehow the peace he'd expected to find upon his return stateside was elusive. It could be because he wasn't actually home yet, in his own bed, surrounded by his own four walls. But he'd thought…

Well, he'd thought Megan would be all the home he'd need.

He watched her trace a line on the map tacked to a corkboard, all business, and wished he had been paying closer attention back in their room. Which underwear did she have on? Was she wearing the sexy stuff made of silk and lace and bright colors?

Or her no-nonsense, white cotton undies that actually turned him on more than the expensive stuff?

Dari rubbed his forehead, surprised at his meandering thoughts.

He'd finally managed to drop off to sleep somewhere around four this morning, only to be jarred awake by the jangling telephone wake-up call an hour and a half later. Megan was already up and in the shower, but when she'd emerged, she'd suggested he sleep in. He told her he intended to jump into this hunt feetfirst, so to speak, so she'd kissed him and told him to meet her here.

Now he watched as she and Jason coordinated new search patterns on the board at the front of the room. He considered joining them up there, but thought it better to glean what details he could before pushing himself into the fray.

A half hour later he felt he had a good handle on the situation. More specifically, that a thorough search had yet to produce any results, so they needed to go back to square one, consider those angles they may have missed. Utilize equipment designed to detect trace evidence.

Someone took the seat next to him. He glanced over to see Linc.

"Hey," Dari greeted.

Linc's response was a nod. "How's it going?"

"It's going." He looked toward the front of the room where the meeting was wrapping up. "Looks like the same applies here."

"Basically."

"Anything the FBI can offer?"

Linc gave him that ghost of a smile that said everything yet nothing.

Darius let it lie. He knew that if there were anything to share, Linc would share it. He was not only a partner of Lazarus Security, he was an important connection to the FBI and other national agencies.

Before he knew it, the morning briefing was breaking up, team members leaving to see to their assigned tasks. Megan came straight to him and asked how he was feeling. He told her he was fine.

"So what do I do?" he asked.

Jason stepped up next to Meg. "You'll be riding shotgun with me." He looked down at where Dari unconsciously rubbed his kneecap. "If you're up for it."

Dari couldn't have gotten up faster, gritting his teeth to mask any pain that accompanied the move. "Man, I was made for it…."

MEGAN STAYED BEHIND in the command center. Though she was the designated contact for the day, she'd have preferred to be out in the field somewhere, doing something to take her mind off…well, everything.

"Oh, I'm sorry. I'll come back to clean up later."

She looked up from the main table tracing the route Search Team #2 would be taking that day to see the motel owner's daughter in the doorway. Megan had seen her before, but only in passing. A quick once-over told Megan the woman was maybe twenty, at least eight months pregnant and unmarried, if her empty ring finger, and lack of any sign that a ring usually occupied the space, was any indication.

She straightened. "That's all right. Do what you need to. You won't bother me."

"Are you sure?"

She nodded, returning her attention to the map in front of her and rearranging her headset as she spoke to the team leader, directing him which direction to go.

"Head east-southeast," she told him. "It'll take you approximately two and a half hours to reach the first clearing…"

A head popped up from the other side of the table. Megan blinked at wide blue eyes and a mop of blond curls. The kid was maybe two…and had taken an open interest in Megan and what she was doing.

A chubby hand appeared slowly and reached for the map.

Megan automatically shifted it to a position of safety, glad that the kid was vertically challenged, not tall enough to bypass her movements without changing position.

"Daisy, leave the nice lady alone," the cleaning girl said.

The two-year-old didn't appear to hear her, making a grunting sound as she tried and failed to reach the map. The name Daisy suited the child with her big, round face and yellow curls.

The girl came over and picked the kid up. "Sorry. My babysitter bailed on me this morning and I had to bring her to work. I would have left her with my mother, but she's got an appointment this morning and can't look after her."

Megan rose to her full height. "That's okay." She extended her hand. "I'm Megan."

The girl looked puzzled for a moment and then chagrined. "Oh! I'm sorry." She began to extend her own hand, saw the yellow rubber glove there, then peeled it off before offering it again. "Dorothy. My, um, parents own the place."

They shook briefly. "You have babysitter probs a lot?" Megan asked, surprised to find herself happy for the distraction from her thoughts.

Dorothy gave an eye roll. "You have no idea. This is my sixth daytime sitter in five months that's proven unreliable." She grimaced. "That's what happens when your resources are limited."

"I imagine." She nodded toward the coffeepot. "You want a cup?"

"Me? Oh, no! I mean, yes, I'd love some, but I don't think it's a good idea. I have a lot to get done this morning." She put the child down again. "Thanks for letting me clean up in here."

"Sure. No problem."

Daisy made a beeline for the table.

"No!" Dorothy reprimanded her.

Megan instantly lifted the map out of reach and found herself smiling at the cherub's devilish expression.

Meg folded the map and placed it out of reach, then took a notepad out instead, turning it to a clean page before reaching for markers.

"You go on ahead and do what you need to do," Megan said to Dorothy. "Daisy and I are just going to do a little drawing."

10

FOLLOWING A TEN-MINUTE DRIVE, Dari climbed out of the passenger's side of the rented SUV with little difficulty despite his temporary cast and took in the scene around him. Jason had driven them to the sheriff's office. He fought a frown. He'd hoped he'd get to see some search duty.

The small Florida town was flat and green and flush with thick forests, a far cry from Colorado Springs. Dari's mind was alive with possibilities of where someone might hide the body of a young girl so she might never be found again.

Even though he had on a standard-issue khaki T-shirt and pants, he might as well have been wearing a fur coat. He was used to the heat, but this wasn't just hot, it was suffocating, even this early in the morning.

Jason came to stand next to him and leaned against the SUV. He lit up a cigarette.

Dari reached for it. "Since when did you take up smoking again?"

His friend moved his hand away. "Since when did you become a nag?"

Dari shifted his weight off his cast, thinking he should have taken his cane out of the car. "I thought you gave them up a couple of years ago after your last tour."

Jason exhaled and flicked the ash off the end of the smoke. "So did I."

Dari remembered clearly because his friend had been hell to live with during the two-month period of the on-again, off-again battle. He'd make it for a week and then buy a pack that would turn into ten before going cold turkey for another week.

"Is this case that trying?"

Jason squinted at him in the hazy early-morning sunlight. "It's not exactly a walk in the forest."

Dari leaned against the car as well, putting the sheriff's office in view. It was little more than a small, squat building that could have been mistaken for an insurance agent or attorney's office.

"That's what I was hoping to do today," he said, not wanting to go inside that building.

"What? Walk in the forest?"

"Yeah."

"With a gimp leg?"

"With a gimp leg."

"You'd only hold me up."

"Oh, yeah? Try me."

Jason pushed off the car and turned his back on the building. "Trust me, I've had my fill of slogging through these swamps. If there was something to be found, we would have found it already."

"Maybe."

"Or maybe not. What are you thinking?"

"I don't know yet." Dari grinned. "I'll let you know when I do."

Jason chuckled and shook his head. "I should have known better than to ask."

"Hey, you know I'm more a man of action. Put me on field duty any day."

"Yeah, me, too."

"Nah, you were always good at working either angle. Actually, from what I've seen over the past year, I think you may have missed your calling. You could have done something to land yourself on the Forbes list."

"Good God, why in the hell would I want to do that?"

"Money, of course. And chicks."

"Money I could always use. But I've never had any trouble in the chick department."

"Speaking of which…anything interesting down here?"

Jason squinted at him but didn't say anything.

This time Dari laughed. "It's not like you to play coy. Don't tell me you went and found discretion."

"It is the better part of valor."

"Never where you're concerned. I usually get the details whether I want them or not."

A sheriff's vehicle pulled up into the lot beside them.

"So, are we planning to go in or just hang out here all day?" Dari asked.

"Get your cane."

"Why?"

Jason gave him a long look.

Dari opened the door and took it out.

"Hey, Savage," the uniformed officer called out as he headed in their direction.

"Sheriff."

The two men shook hands, said something obvious about the oppressive heat and then Jason turned toward Dari.

"Sheriff Harry Brown, I'd like you to meet one of my partners at Lazarus Security, Darius Folsom."

Dari shook the man's hand, noticing the way he looked him over.

Jason added, "Dari's just back from Afghanistan. IED action. Injury leave."

The sheriff's brows hiked up on his forehead. "Rally? Which branch?"

Dari told him.

The other man hiked up his pants. "I'm a Marine myself. And my son's over there now. Kandahar."

"Tough duty," Dari said.

"You bet your ass."

They talked for a few moments more and then

the sheriff said, "It's getting hot as Hades out here. What's say we go inside? I've got some info you guys might be able to use."

Jason winked at Dari as they followed the other man across the lot toward the building. If he didn't know better, he'd say his buddy had set up everything from the word go, from hanging outside at the SUV, to bringing Dari along for the ride, down to the cane he'd asked him to get. And as such, he'd gotten offered information rather than begging for some he'd likely never get.

Dari shook his head. Jason had definitely missed his calling.

UNFORTUNATELY, AN HOUR of small talk had yielded them little more than they already had judging by Jason's disappointed expression. Dari followed him back outside after accepting another cup of coffee the sheriff brewed himself from beans he chose and ground.

As soon as the door closed behind them, Dari said, "I take it he didn't give you anything we can use."

"You take right." Jason let out a long breath, not any happier than Dari at being caught inside—no matter how air-conditioned—wasting precious time. "I already knew the other volunteer search teams had turned up nothing and had been suspended until some of this blasted water dries up. As for the mother and her possible involvement...well, it's little more than glorified gossip at this point without any solid evidence."

They got into the SUV and Jason started it up, blasting the air.

"Do you think they have it?" Dari asked.

"What, solid evidence?" Jason shook his head. "If they did, they would have arrested her already. Or at least pulled her in for official questioning."

"What do Linc and the FBI have to say?"

"Unfortunately much the same as you heard in there. They've already pulled teams back to Quantico."

"So essentially, we're the only ones still actively working the case at this point."

"That'd be about right."

"On our own dime."

"Yep. Unless we turn something up."

"Is there any talk about cutting our own losses and going home?"

"You mean turn tail and run?"

Dari grinned at the saying.

"Not a word. Yet." He glanced at his watch. "I figure we have a good week before we run out of options. Until then…"

"We keep spinning our wheels."

Jason squinted at him. "We keep trying to find the girl. Hopefully alive."

Dari considered him silently. He was mildly surprised his friend held out hope Finley might still be alive. Jason Savage had never been the hopeful type.

It was reality and odds all the way. And the odds in this particular case said that if the girl was lost or had been abandoned somewhere, she'd have been dead a few days ago, just from dehydration and exposure to the elements alone.

If someone still had her...well, then they wouldn't be finding her in any forests. And while Amber Alerts were still being aired, and tips called in and followed up on, it wasn't part of the Lazarus team's job.

A cell phone buzzed.

He checked his, then watched as Jason answered his own.

"Hey," he said simply.

Dari settled back in the seat, scanning the trees on either side of the road.

"We'll meet you there."

He disconnected.

"What is it?" Dari asked.

"That was Megan. Our team found the girl's bike...."

MEGAN HAD BEEN ON the scene for five minutes before Jason and Dari arrived.

The radio call had come in while she was busy with Daisy. He was simple and to the point: "Got it."

Team #2 had been assigned to retrace their steps from the first day, only a few yards to the east. An hour in, they literally stumbled across a girl's pink bicycle mostly submerged under a foot of murky standing rainwater, one handlebar bearing a white-and-pink plastic tassel attached to the end.

Due to forensics concerns, they left the bike where it was, not touching it beyond the initial lift to verify it was what they thought it was and to take photos.

Now they all stood at the tree line waiting for the sheriff's office and FBI forensics team to show up.

"Is it hers?" Jason asked, coming to stand next to Megan.

She relayed the news to the other team. "It looks like it," she said. "Do you think I should pull the other team?"

He appeared to think for a moment. "No. This may be a decoy and the girl was never even in these woods. Tell them to push on. Maybe it will give them added incentive now we've finally found something concrete."

Megan grimaced. "You mean like the fact that we know the girl and her bike weren't beamed up by aliens?"

"Something like that."

She passed on the command and then refastened the radio to her belt.

"Sheriff on his way?" Jason asked.

She nodded. "As is the FBI forensics team. I pulled everyone out of this area until they're finished."

She looked beyond him to where Dari stood at the edge of the forest looking inside. He appeared... oddly detached somehow.

Jason asked, "What's the ID on the bike?"

"Same make, color, tassels. Oh, and the plate has her name on it."

"Finley's not a common name."

"No, it's not."

They shared a look.

If the girl went missing in here, chances were...

She shivered despite the heat. Changing the subject, she asked, "How is he?" She nodded toward Dari.

"Who? Oh, Dari? Good. He's got the sheriff eating out of his hand."

She smiled. "He's good at that."

"Yes, but don't tell him, he'll only call you a liar."

She laughed and then looked to find Dari watching, his gaze moving from her to Jason and back again.

The smile instantly left her face.

He knows...

She wasn't sure where the thought came from, or what she should do about it. But she was suddenly very certain that he knew there was something going on between her and Jason.

Correction: there had been something between them.

11

LATER THAT EVENING, everyone was gathered in the command center sharing their stories of the day, catching dinner, indulging in a brew and enjoying a general atmosphere of relief and accomplishment—their efforts had finally yielded something, even though it wasn't what they'd have liked, which was to find Finley Szymanski alive and well. But now that they'd found some solid evidence, they would be paid for their time in Florida.

And the presence of the bike indicated that they were advancing in the right direction, that they'd been correct in pushing ahead when everyone else had stopped looking.

Finley's mother and grandparents had, indeed, verified that the bike belonged to the little girl and was the one she'd been riding at the time of her disappearance. Unfortunately Linc told them Forensics was pretty sure there would be little available by way of trace evidence, considering it had been pretty well submerged in water. And while it wasn't impossible that the girl had walked the bike that far into the forest, she definitely hadn't ridden it. Meaning they were leaning more toward the "red herring" line of thinking—that there was, indeed, someone else involved in her disappearance and they'd hidden her bike there purposely to throw anyone looking off the true trail.

Megan decided she didn't want to think about that as she knocked back another good swallow of beer, watching Dari across the room where he sat talking to Linc.

He hadn't said more than two words to her since meeting up at the evidence scene. He appeared preoccupied and in more than a little pain.

Jason appeared at her elbow. "Sheriff says he's again acting as go-between for the Szymanskis. Guess the FBI and that slimy lawyer they hired pissed the family off."

"Again."

He smiled. "Again."

Her gaze was glued to Dari's.

"Hey, everything all right?"

She slowly looked at him. "You tell me."

He eyed those around them, enough within hearing range not to take the conversation too far. "If you're asking what I think you are, everything's fine. Nothing on this end."

She exhaled, but not fully. Something was up. She just wasn't sure what yet.

"I think he's in pain," Jason said.

"Yeah, me, too. Not that he'll cop to it."

"Or take the pain pills I'm sure he has."

"We both know why…"

"Yeah. We do."

She turned toward Jason. "Do you think he's looking at us…oddly?"

"Oddly?"

"You know…"

"No. I don't think he's looking at us oddly. He has no reason to."

She nodded. "Right."

"I think you're letting your mind run away with you, McGowan. Reel it back in. Trust me. Everything will be okay."

A COUPLE OF HOURS later back in her motel room, Megan tried to focus on Jason's words, but the more she tried, the blurrier they became.

She spent as much time in the bathroom as she could possibly squeeze out. She showered, shaved, dried her hair, moisturized…and then sat down on the closed toilet trying to gather up her courage to go out in the other room where Dari waited.

She pressed her fingertips against her eyelids. She'd pitted hope against hope that Jason was right and the passage of time would make the situation easier. Instead her guilt seemed to be getting worse. Every time she looked at Dari, the darkness in her expanded. She'd never dealt with an emotion of this nature and figured that had a lot to do with it.

What she didn't know was what to do about it. This…pretending nothing was wrong was not working, no way, no how.

If only the incident hadn't involved someone else close to Dari.

She increased the pressure against her eyelids until she saw stars and then moved her hands away. If the person with whom she'd been unfaithful had been a stranger, this would be so much easier.

Easy. Not a word to be used anywhere in conjunction with her life at the moment.

Still, she had to consider Jason and his friendship with Dari. If this blew up in their faces…

She pushed from the commode and paced the short length of the bathroom then back again.

A rap on the door. "Meggie? You okay in there?"

"What? Oh. Yeah. Be right out."

She bit down hard on her bottom lip, listening for Dari to move away from the door. Then she took a deep breath and went into the other room.

He was limping toward one of the two uncomfortable chairs on either side of a small table near the open window. Like her, he didn't care for the air conditioner, preferring to leave it off until it was time to go to bed.

Megan's gaze drifted to the bed in question.

"Did you need the bathroom?" she asked.

He winced as he sat down. "Nah. I took a shower earlier."

She nodded as she went about the task of putting her laundry into a bag and then stowed it back in the small closet.

"Have you taken something for that?" she asked, gesturing toward where he kneaded his leg above the cast.

He shook his head.

She went into the bathroom and collected ibuprofen along with a glass of water, then took them to him.

"Thanks."

She sat down in the chair opposite him. It was only nine-thirty and the sun had just set, leaving enough light filtering in through the window that they didn't need a lamp yet. The eerie, dim orange glow seemed fitting somehow; surreal.

"So," he said, placing the water glass on the table next to her notes. "Linc called while you were showering. Forensics think they've got a partial thumbprint. And it doesn't match the kid, mom or grandparents."

"Good. That's good. Did they run it through the database?"

"No match."

She reached for the pen next to her notes and wrote down the information. "Both good and bad. Good that no known offender took her. Bad in that we don't know who did."

"If anyone did."

She nodded. "Right."

While chances might be small, they still remained that Finley had walked her bike into that forest for some godforsaken reason and had pushed forward on foot.

Dari took another sip of water. "All search teams resume tomorrow at daybreak."

Another turn with both positive and negative consequences. Good because the more people actively looking for the girl, the greater the chances of finding her. And, ironically, bad for the same reason. The more people who looked for her, the greater the chances that the seasoned pros would be distracted by amateur searchers.

Dari cleared his throat. "Jason and I thought it might be a good idea to get a jump on the others."

She nodded. "Send our teams out before the others get there."

"I'm going out with Team #1."

She squinted at him. "Are you sure you're up for it?"

"I'm sure."

She glanced at where he rubbed his leg again.

"At the first sign I'm holding anyone back, I'll get out."

"Fair enough."

She got up and crossed to the small refrigerator in the corner, taking out a soda and popping the top. "You want one?"

"No. But I'll take a sip of yours."

She smiled and offered it to him before taking a sip. He smiled back and drank, nearly emptying it in one gulp.

She laughed. "Smart-ass."

She got another soda, standing as she drank from it. It was almost unbearably hot. Despite her shower, she was again drenched in sweat. But she'd gotten used to it at some point during their time here.

"Shall I turn on the air?" Dari asked, noticing the way she wiped her forehead with the back of her hand.

She considered him quietly. "Depends."

"On what?"

"On whether you're ready to go to bed."

The grin returned. "To sleep, you mean."

"Mmm. To sleep."

A slow burn began in her stomach and swirled outward.

"Nothing else?"

She opened her eyes innocently. "Are you accusing me of trying to seduce you, Mr. Folsom?"

"No. Just hoping you will."

She pressed the cold soda can against her neck. "Oh, I think that's pretty much guaranteed."

He pushed from the chair and came to stand in front of her. He stood at least five inches taller and she tilted her chin to gaze into his handsome face awash in the fading orange light from the sunset filtering in through the window. Anyone outside wouldn't be able to see inside. At least not yet. For the time being, they'd get the reflection of the setting sun.

He lifted a hand to the side of her face. Megan's eyes drifted closed and she leaned into his touch, her heart beating thickly in her chest. In that one moment she felt more love for him than she'd ever believed herself capable of feeling. He rubbed his thumb across her bottom lip and then a moment later followed with his own lips. He kissed her leisurely, lingering at the corners of her mouth before making his way back to the middle.

Oh, how she'd missed being kissed by him. That was one thing that nothing could take from her... from them.

She reached up, framing his face with her fingers, probing the familiar planes and angles, reveling in the stubble on his chin, the silkiness of his brows, the rough texture of his hair against her skin.

"I love you."

Her whispered words came straight from the heart and left an ache that lodged firmly in her chest.

Regret and guilt and love and need bled together deep within her, making her dizzy with the intensity. She stepped closer, pressing her body into his. The only time she felt a hundred percent okay was when he was inside her, forcing everything else out.

She budged her hand down his chest and stomach until she found the outline of his erection through the thick khaki of his pants.

He groaned into her mouth.

With quick movement, she opened the catch and pushed his pants down, careful not to cause him more pain as she maneuvered around his cast. Then she jerked his T-shirt up over his head, flinging it to land on the other side of the room even as he worked his fingers up under her tank, cupping her breasts in his palms.

Air hissed through her lips as he gently plucked her tight nipples and then bent to run his tongue along the length of one breast, then the other.

Desire rushed through her bloodstream and then back again, coalescing in a deep pool between her thighs.

The shadow of someone walking past the window reminded them the possibility of being seen existed. Dari leaned slightly away, stripping her of her tank before moving to close the curtains and switch on the air conditioner while she checked to make sure the door was locked as she stepped out of her own pants.

They faced each other and Megan couldn't help thinking they weren't merely physically naked, but emotionally as well.

This was one place she didn't have to pretend. She loved Dari. With all her heart. She had from the first moment their eyes met. And she loved him even more now.

She allowed that to show as she gazed at him in the dim light.

She wasn't aware he had moved until she felt the back of his knuckles graze against her sex.

She gasped, automatically spreading her thighs to allow him better access.

He didn't disappoint. He turned his hand around, stroking the length of her swollen flesh with his fingertips before dipping one into her slick opening and then rubbing her own juices over her throbbing clit.

"Yes," she whispered, dropping her head back and losing herself in sheer emotion....

12

THERE WERE TIMES when Dari touched Megan that he thought he might spontaneously combust. On her face, he witnessed such naked emotion he felt compelled to look away, but couldn't. Never had he shared such a connection with another human being before. And during those few violent moments in the Afghan mountains, he was afraid he never would again.

That she was standing before him now, stripped of clothes and pretense…he knew he was the luckiest man on the face of the earth. Not just because he was with her physically, but because she opened to him in a way that set off a series of emotions he couldn't begin to identify but which took him to a place he sometimes wished he never had to leave.

She bore down against his hand where he stroked her wetness. She was always so ready for him it was often difficult to suppress the desire to thrust into her to the hilt, forgoing foreplay altogether. But he loved to watch her face when he took his time with her.

Speaking of which…

He leaned back and with his free hand, switched on the lamp, sending her shadowy form into soft relief.

She blinked and turned her head away. "Do we need that?"

He squinted. She'd never objected before. In fact, she was more often the one to reach for the light.

"I want to see you," he said.

He watched her swallow and tilted her chin toward him even as he removed his fingers from between her legs. Still, she refused to meet his gaze.

He knew a moment of fear. An alarm not much different from the one that had shot through him right before the translator stepped on that IED.

Then she raised her eyes to his and he instantly relaxed. "You always were a perv," she whispered.

He smiled and then kissed her deeply, not stopping until she melted against him, her nipples pressed against the wall of his chest, her hips swaying against his.

Before he met Megan, he'd thought he knew what love was. He'd been in three long-term relationships and nearly married his high-school sweetheart. But what he'd found with Meg…well, everything that came before paled horribly by comparison. She made him feel as if he'd sprouted wings and could fly.

But he'd sensed a distance in her since his return.

He had several Marine buddies who had suffered

the ultimate in separation: the death of love. In many cases, absence didn't make the heart grow fonder, it made it grow cold.

He'd seen it happen on both sides.

Then there's what went down when an injury was involved…

No matter how serious, often the very real possibility of death sometimes caused a loved one to react in self-defense.

He'd never seen any of it happening to him and Megan. They were both veterans of some of the most hellish military actions. They'd forged their relationship during one of them. Witnessed what happened to others. And as such, could safeguard themselves, their relationship, from suffering the same fate.

But there were times since his return he swore she was avoiding him. Then they'd be alone and he knew he still had her heart.

Her fingers snaked around his erection, causing his breath to hiss between his teeth. Did she have any idea how profoundly she affected him? He used to think she did. Before he left. Now…he wasn't so sure. It was as if she held everything that was him in her capable, probing palm—to nurture…or destroy.

"How's your leg?" she whispered.

He swallowed hard, barely capable of thought when she touched him like that. "What leg?"

She smiled.

Dari groaned and grasped her hips, lifting her to lie across the bed where he followed. She spread her thighs wide and he fit perfectly there, his pulsing length cradled in her slick folds. But he resisted the desire to breach her threshold, no matter how much she wriggled and tried to encourage penetration.

Instead, he kissed her deeply, stroking her hair back from her beautiful face, then ran his lips along the line of her brow, down over the curve of her cheek, tracing the outline of her collarbone, then dipped lower to draw a taut nipple into his mouth...

Megan immediately let her approval be known, bucking her hips off the mattress and renewing her search for a deeper meeting.

Dari grasped her hips, holding her still while he dropped wet kisses along her trembling stomach until he was where he'd planned to be all along....

Her sweet, musky scent filled his senses as he used his thumbs to part her swollen folds, revealing the pink, delicate flesh just beneath. He fastened his lips to the tight nub of her clit, and flicked his tongue back and forth. She moaned and twisted the bedsheets in her fists, coming almost immediately.

Rather than abandoning her, he laved her leisurely, prolonging her crisis, reveling in the shivers that continued to ripple through her muscles. Only when she was completely relaxed again did he lick his way back up to kiss her.

She draped her arms around his waist, pulling him close. "What you do to me..."

He pulled back slightly. "If it's a fraction of what you do to me, then it's impressive, indeed."

She smiled and kissed his neck, shifting her hips so that his almost painful erection was cradled in her dampness.

"Are you sure you're ready?" he asked.

"Baby, for you, I'm always ready."

That's all the incentive he needed.

Grabbing a condom from the nightstand, he sheathed himself and positioned the head of his shaft against her tight portal. She bore upward, taking in an inch. He gladly sank slowly up to the hilt.

Sweet angels, she felt so damn good. Tight and wet and responsive. There was no place on earth he felt this way, nowhere else he'd rather be than right here, her soft muscles contracting around his thick hardness. He withdrew and sank down again, pain forgotten, doubt erased, leaving nothing but pure, hot sensation in its wake.

Megan crossed her legs behind his back and tilted her hips forward, taking him in deeper still.

"Yes…"

The whispered word coming from her lips sent his blood pressure soaring. He increased the rhythm of his strokes, not wanting to rush it, but unable to help himself.

She ran her fingernails down his back and cupped his backside, hungrily meeting him thrust for thrust, her breasts swaying with each move. He leaned down to kiss her and paused, counting backward from ten to ward off his crisis. But when she ground upward against him, he groaned, holding her still as he thrust into her again…and again…

"Oh, yes, baby, yes," she whispered, shuddering around him.

Dari strained to keep up the rhythm as the force of his own climax hit him hard, threatening to paralyze his movements. Somehow he managed to keep up, riding the billowing waves, continuing even after she'd gone still, and his own shuddering subsided.

"I love you," he murmured.

Her arms tightened around him. "I love you more."

That's when the moment he'd been waiting for presented itself. He'd thought about it nonstop since the ability to think at all was nearly stolen from him.

Reaching for his pants, he took out the velvet pouch in his pocket, wishing he could have gotten the box he'd wanted first, but not willing to wait another moment.

She watched him through the fringe of her lashes. "What are you doing?"

"Hush and give me a minute."

He awkwardly got down on one knee next to the bed. By now she was curious enough that she moved to a sitting position, staring at him quizzically.

"Dari?"

"Not yet."

He closed his eyes, summoning the words he'd imagined he'd say. But he found them hard to come by.

He smiled and gazed into her shocked face as

he raised the velvet pouch. "From the moment that IED exploded, all I could think of was you, Megan," he said quietly. "And the fact that I'd never told you how I felt." He chuckled. "Okay, maybe I mean I've never showed you." He took the three-carat diamond solitaire from the pouch. "Never officially asked you to be my wife."

She looked so surprised he wondered if she'd heard a single word he'd said.

Then she launched herself into his arms.

After a few moments, he pulled back so he could kiss her and was startled to find her cheeks damp.

She was crying.

He knew a moment of fear so profound he didn't know quite what to do with it.

"Megan? Are you okay?"

SHE WAS OVERWHELMED...

Megan crawled back up into the bed and rolled onto her side, curling up into a semi-fetal position, laid completely bare by Dari's lovemaking—*and* his impromptu proposal. All barriers tumbled down. She was unable to hide from him anymore. Especially when she saw the pained expression on his handsome face, the tenderness and concern in his eyes.

It was ironic somehow that the very elements that had brought them together two and a half years ago were now what threatened to pull them apart. In the swirling chaos of violence, Dari had emerged a rock to which she could cling. He'd grounded her when she was afraid she might rocket away from all that made her human. Reminded her what it was like to touch, taught her what it meant to love.

Introduced her to a feminine, nurturing part of herself she had never known existed much less explored.

A wartime romance with a modern twist. An intense fling. That's what she'd tried to label their time together overseas. She certainly hadn't expected it to last beyond a return stateside.

Not only had they lasted, they'd bonded even further, becoming a true couple in every sense of the word. She'd often felt that where he left off, she began. Instantly related to every corny word of every love song she'd once taken great pleasure at scoffing.

Understood why her father had loved her mother so completely, even long after her death—at the expense of having any meaningful relationship with his only child, his daughter.

And here she had gone and destroyed it...

"What is it? What's the matter?"

She shook her head, incapable of words.

He curved against her back, holding her close. She held tightly on to where his arms were wrapped around her, wishing they could stay like that forever...

Afraid that she didn't have long before they were gone altogether...

13

THE FOLLOWING DAY Dari was so distracted by his worry for Megan, he barely noticed the throbbing of his leg. He and Jason were paired up again. Despite his contention that he could lead a search team on his own, his old pal and partner insisted that they go out together.

He didn't argue.

They were all on the outskirts of their search sites just before dawn, the sky above the color of an old bruise. He and Jason and a couple of the more experienced Lazarus members were to follow a path close to where the girl's bike was found. The others had been placed at twenty-yard intervals. It was a pretty good bet that the sheriff's deputies would be arranging for citizen volunteers to search the same area, so they wanted to get a head start.

As for the FBI, Linc had indicated that they'd already swept and cleared the area, turning up no further evidence. But their search area had been limited, so the Lazarus team was to assume that something still might turn up.

They were two hours in and the sun had fully risen, turning even the forest air stale and hot. They passed the place where the bike had been found some time ago and he and Jason kept close while the other two team members were some yards ahead.

"You okay?" Jason asked.

Dari's back teeth ground together. "I wish everyone would stop asking me that."

His friend raised his hands. "Hey, excuse me all to hell and back for caring."

Dari grimaced, fighting to concentrate on the area around him. There was still far too much standing water around for his liking. Some areas were covered up to his shins, making for slow going and impossible search conditions. Anything could be under the murky surface. And the chance existed that their tramping might send a key piece of evidence deeper into the muck at the bottom.

"Sorry," he muttered. "Didn't mean to bite your head off."

"No harm no foul. So long as you answer my question."

Dari stretched his neck, using an expandable metal poker, not unlike those used by people who collected litter to probe the deeper puddles.

"It's not me I'm worried about," he said quietly.

Jason didn't immediately respond, so he thought maybe he hadn't heard him. Which was just as well.

He'd never been one to discuss personal problems with friends or family.

"It's Megan," he continued without planning to.

Jason looked at him.

"She's… I don't know. Something's wrong. I don't know what. I'm almost afraid to ask, but…"

His friend remained silent as they made slow but steady progress.

"Something's not right."

"I'm sure everything's fine," Jason said. "She's happy to have you back."

"And I'm happy to be back. Despite the circumstances. But…"

Jason chuckled as he checked under a low-hanging branch. "What's the saying? Don't look a gift horse in the mouth?"

That made him smile. "Doesn't that refer to bad dental care?"

"More your area."

"Kind of like not asking an attractive woman with bad teeth to smile."

His friend gave an exaggerated shiver. "God, makes me think of that one girl in Omaha. Remember?"

"I remember you bitching about it. I also remember it didn't stop you from sleeping with her."

His friend went silent.

They continued their forward movement without speaking for a few minutes.

Then Dari cleared his throat. "Did something happen while I was away?"

Jason stared at him. "What do you mean?"

He shrugged and watched his footing through a patch that was flooded to his knees. His right foot hit something and he winced. "With Megan. Did something happen?"

"I'm not sure what you mean."

He shrugged. "I don't know. Did you notice anything different while I was away?"

"She missed the hell out of you. I know that. And she pretty much shut herself off from everything else outside work."

"Really?"

"Really, what? That she missed you?"

"No. That she shut herself off from everything."

"Yeah. It surprised me, too." They were close enough that Jason slapped his hand on his shoulder. "I'm sure she'll be fine. Probably emotional overload. You know chicks. Your being hurt. Coming home. This case and the odds of the girl being found alive dwindling. Hell, isn't there a full moon tonight?"

He chuckled. "Then there's that."

They fell silent again. But what refused to be quieted was the small voice in the back of his head telling him something was wrong. And it wouldn't be right again until he found out what it was.

LATER THAT EVENING, Megan cleared the dinner wrappers in the command center. None of the search teams—theirs or the sheriff's—had turned up anything noteworthy. Dari had gone with Linc and a couple of the guys to catch a beer at a nearby bar. Seeing as it was a Friday, most of the team had done the same, leaving her and a couple of stragglers behind. And now even they had left.

She'd been relieved when Dari had agreed to join the guys for a beer. Ever since last night she'd been an emotional wreck. While there had been hope that time might heal all before, after crying in front of him she knew he'd be like a dog with a bone between his teeth. And the way he looked at her now...

She swallowed hard.

Distracting him with sex had been a great idea. Right. What she hadn't counted on was what would happen when they made love.

Or when he proposed.

She'd found the exquisite diamond ring he'd tried to give her on the bedside table along with a note: "You don't have to give me an answer now. Keep this until you do." Signed simply, "Dari."

She'd packed the ring in with her gear to keep it safe after sitting staring at it for a long time, not daring to put it on.

"Mind telling me what's going on?"

Megan slowed her movements as she tied off the garbage bag at the sound of Jason's voice behind her. She took the bag to the door where she'd put it in the Dumpster outside later.

"With what?" she asked.

"What in the hell did you say to Dari last night?"

She averted her gaze and felt her face go red. "I

didn't say anything." Which was true enough. She hadn't been able to say a word—she'd been too choked up. Then she'd cried herself to sleep and woke up to find him in the shower, giving her the opportunity to duck out of the room and get straight to work.

She hadn't been alone with him since. And she wasn't looking forward to when she would be.

"Well, something happened because he grilled me to no end today."

She stared at him, her heart doing a triple beat in her chest.

"No, no, nothing like that. He says he knows something's wrong with you and was trying to see if I knew what it might be."

"Are you sure he doesn't suspect…?"

"Positive. If he did, I wouldn't have been grilled, I'd have been eaten raw."

Megan leaned against the main table and briefly closed her eyes. "What did you say?"

Jason didn't immediately respond. Restlessness coated her stomach.

"You know, never mind. Don't answer that." She pushed from the table and paced. "This… You and I just talking like this feels like a betrayal."

"We didn't betray him."

"How can you say that? Of course we betrayed him!"

"Now you're just talking stupid."

She'd never seen Jason so upset before. At least not with her.

"He and I are a couple," she said. "Any relations outside that sphere is a betrayal. It doesn't matter that we didn't kiss. Or that we made a point of not looking at each other. It was infidelity, pure and simple."

"It was sex. Nothing more."

"Well, when you put it that way…" She closed her eyes and took a deep breath. "I'm going to tell him. I have no other choice. Not now that he knows something's wrong."

"Damn it! Don't I have a say in the matter?"

He paced across the room and then back again, looking like a caged animal desperate to escape.

"Don't worry. I won't say it was you."

He stared at her. "Right. You're going to tell him that you slept with some random stranger."

She crossed her arms. "That's right."

"And you'll do that because…?"

"Because you're too big of a coward to fess up yourself."

She began to walk away, firm in her decision. He grasped her arm a little roughly.

At least six ways to take him down leaped to mind; she suppressed all of them. He wouldn't hurt her. She knew that. Just because he overreacted didn't mean she was justified in doing the same.

At least not in a way that she hadn't already volunteered to.

He took a deep breath and released her. "Sorry."

She didn't say anything.

"I just don't understand how telling him is going to make anything better."

"It will clear my conscience."

"And rip his heart clean out of his chest."

She winced at that.

The last thing she wanted to do was hurt Dari. But she couldn't keep this from him any longer.

"Look," Jason said quietly, "he's the best friend I've ever had. My only true friend, if you want to know the truth. If you tell him…"

She searched his face, relating all too closely to what he was saying. Dari was her first love. Her only love. To jeopardize all that because of one night that didn't mean anything to her beyond physical release…

Well, she should have thought about that before she did it, a small voice in her head said.

"Do what you need to do," Jason said finally.

He turned and strode toward the door.

"I meant what I said," she whispered. "I won't mention it was you if you don't want me to. I have a feeling he won't even ask."

He stopped midstep. "Trust me—it will be the first question out of his mouth." He looked over his shoulder. "And if you're going to tell him the truth, then tell him the whole truth. The way I see it, you're not going to rest until he knows everything anyway. Better to do it in one shot than drag it out."

Seeing the logic in his words, she opened her

mouth to say something. Only, he was out the door before she could put her thoughts together.

OF COURSE, THE INSTANT she'd made the decision, the opportunity to tell him was denied her at every turn. That night, he'd come back so late she'd been asleep when he'd entered the room. The next morning, she'd woken to an insistent knock, one of the team members needing to return home due to a family emergency.

Now it was Sunday morning, and everyone had suspended their searches due to the weather; Mother Nature seemed to be hell-bent on reclaiming the already soggy mass of land and giving it back to the sea.

Midmorning, Megan was in the command center reviewing the search map, a couple of other team members milling around, drinking coffee and shooting the breeze. Dari, Jason and Linc had gone to meet up at the sheriff's office to see if they couldn't scare up any additional information at the sheriff's invitation. They'd taken doughnuts with them as an incentive.

With a sigh, she tucked the map under her other papers and reviewed the evidence so far: bike, partial thumbprint, the last time she was spotted, interviews. Nothing jumped out at her.

Of course, it would help if her thoughts didn't keep returning to Dari and how he was going to react to her news when she finally told him.

There was a squeal that could no how, no way, be attributed to any of the team members in the room. She looked up to find little Daisy skipping into the room in a pretty yellow dress, her blond curls brushed to a bouncy sheen. She made a beeline to the table Megan sat behind, her smile as big as the state.

"Megan!" she exclaimed.

Megan couldn't help smiling. "Good morning, Daisy. You look very pretty this morning."

The girl grabbed her skirt and lifted it up, revealing her thick training pants.

Dorothy was on her heels, looking pretty herself in a light blue dress. "Daisy, put your dress down. How many times do I have to tell you it's not polite to flash your underpants to total strangers?"

One of the male team members in the corner chuckled, "Actually, it makes things simple."

The two women shared an eye roll even as Dorothy smoothed her daughter's dress back where it belonged.

"Something special today?" Megan asked.

"No, just church," Dorothy said. "We're leaving as soon as I straighten up a little in here."

"There's nothing that can't wait," Megan told her. "Which church?"

She named the same church to which the Szymanski family belonged.

"Would you like to come along?" Dorothy asked, her face lighting up.

Megan intended to instantly refuse, then thought

again. "Actually, that might be just what the doctor ordered," she said quietly. "Can you give me a few minutes to change? I don't have a dress, but I think I can scare up something suitable…."

14

DARI SHOOK HANDS with the sheriff last, nodding as Jason led the way out of the office, Linc following closely behind. Beyond learning which areas the volunteers had searched, and a follow-up interview with the girl's mother that may or may not offer up any additional clues, the meeting hadn't yielded much by way of evidence. As usual, Linc had remained quiet throughout, seeming to blend in with the background. Dari knew it was probably part of his training, but still, he marveled at how successful the big man was at disappearing in full sight. He suspected Linc could have gotten up and searched the sheriff's desk drawers with the man sitting right there and no one would have thought anything about it.

Jason, on the other hand, had leaned toward the short-tempered side. Atypical behavior that had drawn Dari's surprised stare on a couple of occasions. In fact, his friend had been acting strangely for the past couple of days. Was the case getting to him? Highly unlikely. Dari had seen Jason in circumstances much more intense than this and he'd never lost his cool. In fact, the more extreme the conditions, the better Jason seemed to function.

"Okay, man, what's up?" Dari asked as they walked toward the SUV, the rain having slowed to a momentary trickle.

Jason shot him an irritated glance. "I could ask the same of you."

Linc stared at them both.

"I'm not following you," Dari said.

"Every time I tried to lead that clueless sheriff in a direction that might prove of some use to us, you cut me off at the pass."

"Did I?" He had no recollection of doing any such thing. "Then why in the hell did you bring me if I'm such a liability?"

"You weren't. Until today."

They climbed into the SUV, Linc automatically getting into the back, once again disappearing into the background.

Jason started the SUV and put it into gear with an angry jerk.

"Whoa," Dari said when he pulled into traffic without looking, earning them a horn blast. "Cool it before you get us all killed."

His words seemed to jerk his friend back from whatever edge he'd been on.

They'd all faced much more dire situations. And

in this case, none of them were on the line physically. It made Jason's surly attitude all the more curious.

They finished the rest of the ride in silence. By the time they returned to the motel, the rain had picked up again, thick sheets that limited visibility and guaranteed you'd be soaked the instant you stepped outside into it.

That didn't stop Dari as he climbed out of the vehicle and headed for the command center. He shook off the wetness and made room for Linc, who came in behind him. Jason, it appeared, had stayed behind in the SUV.

He greeted the two team members playing cards in the corner and scanned the rest of the room. "Where's Meg?"

"I don't know. She went someplace with that girl who cleans up after us."

He frowned. Why would she leave without giving him at least a call to let him know where she was going?

He turned back toward the door, looking at the torrent and catching the taillights of Jason's SUV as he sped out of the parking lot back into traffic.

Now where in the hell was he going?

He took out his cell phone and dialed Megan's number. She didn't answer.

"Damn."

"Problems?" Linc asked.

"Huh? No." He slid his cell back into his pocket and asked, "You any good at Texas hold 'em?"

Linc grinned. "I've been known to win a few."

He chuckled. "I bet." He looked toward the two in the corner. "Got room for a couple more?"

THE MISERABLE WEATHER didn't keep churchgoers away from Sunday services. The chapel was bursting at the seams, with even more people spilling out the open doors, down the stairs and into the parking lot, umbrellas keeping them safe from most of the rain.

Megan and Dorothy arrived early enough to get spots in one of the back bench seats. While air-conditioning made the interior bearable, being near the open doors meant a swing back and forth from cool to warm and back again.

Megan plucked her white blouse from where it stuck to her chest, as much from sweat as from the rain that had soaked her in the mad dash from the car to the chapel, leaving the umbrella more for Dorothy and Daisy. She'd changed into the only civilian clothes she'd brought along to Florida, which consisted of a pair of black slacks, a white blouse and black pumps. She'd pulled her hair back into a twist and even now felt rivulets of sweat trickling down the back of her neck. She could barely make out what the pastor was saying over the sound of flapping papers as others fanned themselves. The service was full of hope that the retrieval of little Finley's bike was a sign that she would be found alive.

The pastor nodded to the front seats. Megan craned her head to see that Finley's mother and grandparents were there, heads bowed, the grandmother openly weeping at the pastor's words.

Dorothy leaned into her. "That's you, right? You found the bike?" she whispered.

Megan looked down. "My team, yes. Not me personally."

"That's great. I don't know what I'd do if my Daisy went missing. They might as well take me out back and shoot me."

Megan raised her brows as she looked at her.

Daisy fidgeted on her mom's lap, a space made smaller yet by the sibling growing there. Dorothy winced and rubbed her very pregnant belly.

Megan turned her attention back to the audience, noticing a few familiar faces—the pastor's family, some volunteer search members, and, to her amazement, a couple from Lazarus's team. She felt a sharp knee on her leg and looked to see Daisy crawling into her lap, apparently finding her mother's lacking. She was all big blue eyes and toothy smile as she looked up at her. Megan couldn't help smiling back as she helped the child settle more comfortably, tucking her against her body, an arm around her to prevent her from falling. Dorothy took the opportunity to focus on the pastor, fanning herself with a church flyer.

The girl relaxed against Megan, popping her thumb into her mouth as she stared at the back of the woman's hat in front of them. Megan tucked her chin in and took a deep breath, enjoying the scents of baby shampoo and little girl.

How long had it been since she'd held a child? She'd babysat for a couple of neighbors when she was a teen, but being an only child, a military brat, and then entering the military straight out of high school, she hadn't been around a lot of kids. Certainly not enough to make her comfortable around them.

Yet it felt completely natural having Daisy on her lap.

She briefly closed her eyes, trying to imagine what it might be like to have children of her own. To have her belly as round as Dorothy's. She hadn't thought about it much before. Oh, maybe she'd entertained the thought every now and again during her relationship with Dari. They'd joked that she'd probably end up with a hyperfeminine little girl given to all things frilly and pink, but she'd never seriously considered having a child. Never thought about what she could offer one. What he or she might offer her.

And she'd never certainly factored in the protectiveness she'd feel. Welcoming Daisy onto her lap, and automatically wrapping her arm around her to keep her safe, inspired myriad emotions, the most prevalent being the need to keep her safe. She'd do anything to protect her.

Anything.

The sermon ended and everyone got up and began milling around.

"Oh, look, it's stopped raining," Dorothy said. "I'm going to take Daisy outside and talk to a couple of friends. Meet you at the car in a bit?"

Megan smiled. "Sure."

She wanted to see if she could approach Finley's family, maybe introduce herself. Her reasons for attending hadn't been entirely personal, despite her growing attachment to the little munchkin and her mother.

She smiled as she wove her way around others trying to make their way out, a bit of a fish swimming upstream, everyone in their Sunday best, hats hitting her left and right, perfume threatening to choke her.

Finally, she was at the front of the chapel. The pastor immediately recognized her.

"Miss McGowan. How nice to see you." He enfolded her hand in both of his, his smile genuine. "I'm glad you could join us for this morning's sermon."

"My compliments," she said.

He turned toward Finley's family. "Have you had a chance to meet one of the people responsible for finding the bicycle?" he asked.

Megan couldn't have asked for a better introduction. She glanced upward, wondering if it was a bit of divine intervention during a time when she could use exactly that.

The first thing that struck her was how young Finley's mother looked. Around the same age as Dorothy, she guessed, but with a seven-year-old daughter who was now missing.

Her parents, on the other hand, looked older than their years.

She greeted each of them one by one, explaining that her team had found the bike, not her specifically, and wishing she could share that they'd found a partial print. And that surprised her, since none of the three had actually been ruled out as possible suspects in the missing girl's disappearance. Still, her gut reaction was that they weren't involved.

Finley's grandfather stepped forward. "I just want to thank you for continuing the search. Everyone else had given up hope, no matter how much we begged otherwise. You guys finding, um, Finley's bike, sparked renewed interest." It was clear he had trouble saying her name without choking up. "Thank God. I don't know what would happen if everyone just gave up…."

Megan said words she hoped were reassuring, not completely at ease being on this side of the equation, but glad she'd played a small role in inspiring hope.

"Please," his wife said, "stop by the house for some coffee or something. We'd like to discuss the details of what you found…"

She was surprised by their generosity and exchanged numbers with them—she already had the address, as did everyone within remote distance of a television set.

Promising to be in contact the following day, she said her goodbyes, thanked the pastor and made her way outside.

It was sprinkling again and the throng of people had dissipated, cars lining up to turn out of the lot into traffic that had grown heavier since they'd arrived.

She immediately spotted Dorothy talking to a couple of other women under three overlapping umbrellas in the corner of the parking lot near her car. She started in that direction, scanning the others who lingered chatting. One of them was familiar. Her steps slowed as she recognized Don McCain. He was crouched over, putting himself eye to eye with Daisy, who giggled at something he said.

Megan's heart gave a triple beat. He had at least four other children in front of him but the image of him, with his hand out offering something to Daisy didn't set well with her. She was filled with the urge to go over and guide the girl away, but suppressed it. Instead, she walked to Dorothy who was laughing at something one of the others had said but was keeping her eye on her daughter.

"Oh, hi!" Dorothy greeted her. "Megan, I'd like you to meet two of my dearest friends in the world."

She made the introductions and Megan was pretty sure she made the appropriate responses, but her gaze was glued to Don McCain and Daisy.

The four of them chatted a bit and then the two women excused themselves, wishing Dorothy and Megan a good day in order to collect their own children and head home to fix dinner.

"What do you know about him?" Megan asked once they were alone.

"Who, Mr. McCain?" She waved a hand. "He's harmless. He sometimes plays the organ for the church and is an elementary-school teacher. He loves kids."

Megan tried to force herself to relax. To explain that all this was new to her. It was one thing to look at somebody objectively, another through the lens of a protective adult.

Or in her case, overprotective adult.

"Daisy?" Dorothy called. "Say goodbye to Mr. McCain. We've got to be going now."

Daisy did as asked, giving Mr. McCain a big hug and a kiss on the cheek before skipping back to them.

Megan felt much better when she was near and was barely able to return the wave McCain offered before they all got into the car.

15

MEGAN RETURNED TO the motel to find Dari playing cards with the guys in the command center. She declined their invitation to join them, went out on a lunch run where she picked herself up some good stir-fry, and then went to her room to enjoy a bit of quiet while she could. Tomorrow and the renewed search would come soon enough.

The impending talk with Dari the same.

She had to appreciate that the imposed delay had provided her with a sense of gravity. Once she'd accepted she needed to tell him, she'd found a bit of peace within herself. Come what may, the truth had to come out. Even if it meant hurting him. Even if it meant losing him.

She still didn't know what she would or wouldn't say about Jason. Could he be right? Would the first question Dari asked be who she'd had sex with?

She figured she'd cross that bridge when she came to it.

Now as she lay across the bed with the latest book from one of her favorite mystery authors, she found herself drifting more than reading. She put the book aside and rolled over, allowing recent events to slide through her mind unchecked. From Dari's alarmed reaction to her crying to holding Daisy in her lap earlier in the chapel.

Having served overseas, she understood that traveling had a way of taking you outside yourself. It forced you to step outside the box of your reality and look at life from a different angle. Sometimes you didn't much like what you saw. Other times, the fresh view served to strengthen your values and your beliefs.

This assignment was a strange mixture of both.

If not for the ceaseless pain in her chest, it might end up being positive in many ways.

She wrapped her arms around herself, hugging tightly, as if to ward off the bad. What she was to face she had to face.

She glanced at the clock on the nightstand. Just past six. The card game could go on for only Lord knew how long. She wondered if Jason had joined them. She hadn't had a chance to speak to him since their words the other day. Did he think she'd already told Dari? She hadn't seen him around earlier, so she couldn't say.

She lifted herself into a sitting position and then crossed her legs before reaching for her cell phone. Scrolling through her phone book for a number she hadn't dialed in a while, she found it and then pressed the call button.

Within two rings her father picked up.

"Dad? Hi, it's Megan."

A brief pause and then, "You don't have to tell me your name, darling. If you're calling me Dad, then it is you."

She smiled and leaned back against the pillows, enjoying the sound of his voice for the first time in what seemed like a long time. Not because she hadn't spoken to him. She tried to call at least once a week. No, she usually didn't enjoy her conversations with him because his saying words like *darling* and *baby* used to upset her.

But holding Daisy earlier, and thinking of the words in connection to her…well, she had a moment of understanding.

And she also experienced a pinprick of hope that she and her father might finally find that patch of common ground that seemed to have eluded them for so long. Ground that they could tentatively start to build on.

DARI WAS DOWN thirty-five dollars, but he figured, in the scheme of things, the amount was paltry compared to what he could have lost. At least two of the guys were down four times that. At any rate, as the day wore on and more of the team members returned to the motel and joined them in the command center, the table and number of players had lengthened and multiplied. There were eight of them playing now, with another four sitting nearby keeping up a lively commentary and the rest well-supplied with beer.

Dari wiped the sweat from his brow with the back of his wrist. The air-conditioning was on but the door was open, the stifling, liquid heat of the day crowding the room. Jason had yet to return, and Dari found himself constantly on the lookout for him. No one knew where he'd gone and a phone call to his cell had gone right to voice mail.

He lost another hand and tossed his cards down in mock upset.

"Lucky in love," Dominic said.

"Unlucky in cards," one of the other guys said.

A string of profanity sounded from the direction of the doorway and they all looked to find Jason coming inside, looking the worse for wear.

"Hey, Savage. Strike out at the bar?" someone called out.

Jason told him to do something that was physically impossible. Dari knocked back the last of his beer, watching his friend. Then he said, "Okay, guys, I'm out."

There was the requisite moaning and groaning, but nothing that stopped Dari from pushing his chair from the table and getting up, the three beers he'd consumed over the past five hours having little impact on him.

Jason, on the other hand, looked as if he had lain with his mouth open under a keg.

"Hey, buddy," Dari said, advancing on his friend. "What's say we get you to your room and into the shower."

Jason stared at him. Dari wondered how many of him he was seeing.

"Did you drive in this condition?"

Linc came inside and jangled the keys. He'd left about an hour or so into the game, destination unknown. Apparently he'd caught up with Jason at whatever bar Dominic had been referring to and had driven him back.

"You all are like a bunch of old hens. Peck, peck, peck," Jason mumbled, going for the minirefrigerator and the beer stocked inside.

Dari closed the door before Jason could get one out. "Looks like you've already had your quota. Come on. Let's go."

"I'm warning you, buster, come between me and my beer one more time and you're going to see just how angry this cock can get…"

Buster? Dari half grinned. The only time Jason used that word was when he was two sheets in.

Dari supposed he should count himself lucky his friend wasn't using anything stronger.

Dari took his arm and tried to lead him away from the refrigerator.

"Hey, man, I said let me go…"

Jason jerked his arm back so erratically he nearly fell straight on his ass, and would have had Dari not helped right him.

"Room," Linc said quietly.

Dari nodded, glad at the offer of help.

Without another word, Dari grabbed Jason's left arm while Linc took his right and they quickly maneuvered him outside.

"Where in the hell are you taking me? What I need is back there."

"What you need is a cold shower and a good night's rest," Dari told him.

Within moments, they were outside Jason's room. Linc took Jason's key from his back pocket and opened the door, but Jason had one good attempt at autonomy left in him and Linc's distraction allowed him to make it. He shook free from them both and stumbled down the curb into the parking lot, where a car was pulling up, headlights cutting duo cones through the heavy rain. Dari reached out and yanked him back out of the way before the car hit him.

"Whoa, buddy. That was close."

"Where in the hell do you think you're going?" Jason railed at the driver.

Dari grabbed the back of his shirt and forced him toward the motel-room door, not stopping until he pushed him into the upright shower stall, where he slipped and fell on his ass.

Linc stood in the doorway. "Got this?"

"Yeah. Thanks, man."

He disappeared and a moment later Dari heard the door close. He reached and turned on the faucet full blast before Jason could regain his footing and make a beeline for the door. He watched as his friend sputtered and cursed, more concerned with trying to get the spray out of his eyes than going anywhere.

Dari couldn't remember a time when he'd seen Jason this deep into a bottle.

"Okay, okay. Enough already," Jason protested.

Dari reached in and switched off the faucet, then handed Jason a towel. He snatched it and dried his face, making no attempt at getting up. He was soaked from head to boot.

"When's the last time you ate?" Dari asked.

Jason blinked at him. "What the hell do you care?"

That's the second time he appeared to question his interest.

Dari helped him to his feet. "Well, then, maybe you should start by telling me what's going on."

Jason nearly slipped getting out of the shower, but shrugged off Dari's attempt to help him. "You already know what's going on."

Dari leaned against the doorjamb, partly to keep his friend from trying to make another run on the beer, mostly because he wanted to hear whatever it was that needed to be said but hadn't been yet. "If I knew, would I be asking?"

Jason stripped out of his T-shirt and awkwardly removed his boots while hopping on one foot.

"Is it what went down at the sheriff's office this morning?" Dari asked.

"The sheriff's… What in the hell are you talking about?"

Dari hadn't thought that was behind whatever was eating his buddy. Rather, whatever was going through Jason's head was to blame for what had happened this morning, as well.

"Then what is it?"

Jason threw his right boot against the wall so hard one of the tiles cracked. "What? Megan told you already, didn't she? So why in the hell are you pretending everything is business as usual?"

Dari felt as if he'd been sucker punched in the stomach. He straightened, bracing himself for something he was no longer sure he wanted to hear.

Jason turned to stare at him. "God, I haven't given you enough credit. You have a great poker face."

"What did Megan tell me?"

For the first time since he'd shown up in the command center, Jason looked semisober.

And none too happy with himself.

He looked away. "Shit…"

16

MEGAN MUST HAVE dropped off to sleep. She woke with a start and jerked to an upright position where she was still dressed on the bed. She realized it must have been the door slamming that had jarred her awake. Dari stood just inside, looking angry and hurt and as if he wanted to hit something.

Her throat tightened.

He knows…

She scooted to the edge of the bed, the book falling to the floor half noticed as she stood to face him.

"Dari…"

"You slept with him? You slept with Jason Savage?"

Oh, God. This was so not the way she saw this conversation happening.

Jason had told him? She couldn't imagine him doing that. Yet here Dari stood, proof that he had.

"We…had…sex. Yes. Once."

He advanced on her, coming to stand mere inches away. "Explain it to me."

"Tell me what Jason told you."

"Why? So you can get your stories straight?"

She winced, recognizing his mistrust as one of the first casualties of his awareness of her sin. "No. So I don't have to repeat what you've already heard."

"To save you from having to say it?"

"No, Dari. To save you from having to hear it."

He looked at her long and hard. She fought to hold his gaze and not look away even though she wanted to dive under the covers and pull a pillow over her head, not to reemerge until the world started making sense again.

Which might be never.

"Dari, I..."

He waited silently.

"I'm sorry." She bit on her bottom lip.

"Who initiated it?" he asked.

"It doesn't matter."

"It does to me."

"Why? It was one time. Over. It didn't mean anything."

She cringed inwardly at the words.

"I'm sorry. Period. I'm not going to try to justify myself. Truth is, there is no justifying it. I know that now."

"Damn it, Megan! How could you do this to me?"

Her voice dropped to a whisper. "I didn't do it to

you, Dari. I did it to myself. I thought I was doing it for myself. I missed you so much. Missed touching you, holding you…"

"Screwing me…"

She swallowed hard. "If it makes any difference at all, there was no intimacy between us. We didn't kiss. We didn't even face each other…"

He winced and looked away, realizing she'd given him a visual she would prefer he not have had. An image she wished she didn't possess.

In that one moment, Megan knew there was nothing she could do, nothing she could say, that would make this easier for him. All she could do was suffer the consequences.

"Trust me, if I could take it back, undo it all, I'd do it in a blink. The last thing I wanted to do was hurt you. To hurt us. I know that doesn't mean much now…"

"Why didn't you tell me straight off?" he asked.

Her heart skipped a beat. What did she say? She decided that from here on out the truth was the only element that held worth.

"I didn't tell you because I agreed I wouldn't."

His eyes narrowed. "Agreed you wouldn't. Agreed with whom? With Savage?"

"That sounds worse than it is, but yes."

He began to turn away from her.

She laid her hand on his arm and he stopped.

"As hard as it may be to believe now, we agreed not to say anything because there was no point in it."

"You were unfaithful."

"With my body? Yes. Not with my heart. Not with my soul."

His gaze could have bored a hole straight through her.

"I needed…something. You were out on patrol. Our last phone conversation was cut off. I was alone…"

"So you screwed my best friend."

If she could jump out of her skin just then, she would have gladly done so. It felt two sizes too small. Uncomfortable. Suffocating.

"Yes."

His expression darkened.

"Look, I told myself I wasn't going to try to justify this. There is no justification. No excuse. I told myself it was just sex, a physical release at a time when so much was going wrong. Nothing more. Nothing less. Jason…"

His hands formed into fists at the use of his friend's name and she knew a moment of fear.

"We, um, decided not to say anything. To ride it out. Treat it like the nonevent it really was."

"Did you enjoy it?"

Of all the questions he could have asked, she would never have expected that one.

She had no answer for him. She couldn't tell him that, yes, she had enjoyed it. Needed it. On a strictly physical level that had nothing to do with her heart.

Instead, she said, "I'm sorry, Dari. Please know…I love you."

"You love me?" He snorted. "You love me? You shared your body with another man. My best friend. How does that in any way demonstrate your love for me?"

He turned.

"Where are you going?" She bit her bottom lip, wanting to reach out for him but not daring to.

He didn't answer. He merely grabbed his duffel, which was always packed, and left, slamming the door behind him.

DARI WISHED HE WERE anywhere but here. He'd trade the most hellacious, dangerous battle zone on God's green earth over having to feel what he was experiencing just then.

He stood outside the motel-room door, his hand raised, then knocked against the hollow metal. Linc opened up as if he'd been standing just on the other side.

He took one look at Dari and stepped aside so he could enter.

Dari did, thanking him.

"Pick either bed. I bunk on the floor."

Dari tossed his duffel on the second one.

"I was just going out. Be back later," Linc said.

Dari sat down on the bed he'd chosen. "Thanks, man."

Linc nodded and then disappeared through the door, leaving him alone with his swirling thoughts. Wondering if he'd ever be able to forgive the woman he'd spent the past two and a half years loving. Forget a face that had seen him through four months of hell on earth.

Forgive a best friend who had committed the worst of all sins….

MEGAN COULDN'T BE SURE how much time had passed as she sat in the middle of the bed, her knees pulled to her chest, rocking. It could have been minutes. It could have been days. She had never cried so much in her life. Had never felt so broken.

She'd never looked out at the future and felt so utterly hopeless, not knowing what came next or if she even cared enough to find out.

She'd known Dari would take the news hard. But somehow she thought it must have been worse coming from Jason.

Yeah, like it would have been any better coming from her.

She clamped her eyes closed and her arms tighter, wishing she could take back the past week, forcing back the hands of time so that she was once again standing in this room opposite Jason. But this time, she had the good sense to turn down his offer.

Her cell phone rang on the bedside table. She stared at it, not daring to hope it could be Darius. She picked it up. Jason.

Three simple words: "They found her."

NO MORE THAN FIVE minutes later everyone was present in the command center. A television had been rolled in and they all watched the news from various positions.

There weren't very many details. Only that a search volunteer had decided to go out on his own when the rain stopped and happened to find her.

"Thank God she's alive," one of the team members said, earning nods from almost everyone in the room.

"Wish we could have found her," another said.

"They're not saying who did."

Jason got up and shut off the TV. "The sheriff's scheduled a press conference for first thing in the morning. I'm going to head over there and see what I can find out now."

He looked toward Dari, who ignored him, arms crossed and looking everywhere but at either Jason or Megan.

"Shotgun," another member said.

She noticed Linc slip from the room without a word, probably to check with his FBI contacts. At any rate, they'd probably know much more than the media in an hour or so. The only thing they'd seen in the news were shots of the front of the family's house and the sheriff's office, both locked up tighter than a clam's buttocks.

Jason left and someone suggested ordering pizza while they waited. Megan looked at Dari. He got up and walked past her without acknowledging her presence.

She considered returning to her own room, and

then thought better of it. What would she do there but cry?

She watched Dari leave the room and felt her eyes well up. What was she talking about? She could very well just break down here.

"Who said something about pizza?" she asked with a false smile. "And who's going out on a beer run? Looks like we're going to have a long night ahead of us…"

17

THE FOLLOWING MORNING, Megan was still in the command center. Even if there was sleep to be had, she knew she wouldn't have gotten any. So she'd stayed there, hoping against hope Dari would return. But he hadn't. Only Jason and Linc had. She'd spoken briefly to Linc but Jason was navigating a wide berth around her and she was doing the same.

That aspect of her life seemed to be in stop-animation right now, on pause. And she didn't know when—or if—it might ever go live again.

Now they were all in front of the television again, pizza and beer replaced by doughnuts and coffee. It was just after 8:00 a.m. The sheriff had held his press conference. And the media were beginning to compile information of their own.

Megan watched video of Don McCain flash across the screen. It was footage that had been taken a few days ago outside the church.

"I still can't believe McCain's the one who found her," Dominic said.

She couldn't believe it either.

"Dumb luck. We should have continued the search nonstop after we found that bike," Jason said. "From what the sheriff said, she was found not far from where we left off the other day."

A couple of the other guys agreed. They should have kept looking. Maybe they would have saved the girl another two days of isolation.

Megan was sitting at the table tapping her pen against her pad. She'd made several notes.

It was said the girl had survived by drinking rainwater and eating berries. She was suffering from malnutrition and exposure but otherwise was in good condition.

"So what do we do now?" Dominic asked.

Jason was at the communal laptop. "I'll have your tickets and boarding passes printed up in a minute. We're going home."

Megan looked at him and for the first time since last night, he returned her gaze.

Home.

If only it were possible for them to go home, to return to the way things used to be. Before this assignment. Before the mess she'd made out of everything.

"Skip mine," she said.

His gaze narrowed.

"I have some things I want to follow up on."

He returned to communicating with the main office where travel arrangements were being made.

Megan would like to say she was happy. Oh, she was enormously relieved Finley had been found alive. That went without saying. But happiness about her life in general was hard to come by. And she seriously wondered if she'd ever achieve it again.

As if on cue, Dari walked in. Dominic stood at the borrowed printer, taking out the boarding passes as quickly as they were generated. He held Dari's out.

"Yours."

He glanced at it and then returned it. "I'm not going back."

Megan and Jason stared at him, but he didn't acknowledge their interest.

He wasn't going back now? Or ever?

Her stomach bottomed out at the thought she might not see him again.

He was a full partner of the company. But as soon as he recovered from his injury, he would be heading back over to Afghanistan again. If not sooner.

If he wasn't going back, where would he be going?

She wanted to ask. But was afraid not only that he wouldn't respond, but that she wouldn't like the answer if he did.

She pushed from the table, gathered her things and headed back to her room.

DARI HAD SPENT THE night staring at the ceiling, dry-eyed and hollow. He'd hoped that by this morning he'd be able to look at Megan without feeling as if she'd ripped his heart out with her bare hands. But he'd been fooling himself. The instant he'd spotted her in the command center, it was yesterday and she was telling him she loved him all over again.

Damn, damn, damn, damn! Why had she done it? Why had Jason?

He stared at the man in question. Scratch that. He knew exactly why Jason had done it. He'd been a pussy hound his entire adult life.

Problem was, he hadn't expected his best friend to go sniffing after his girl.

He winced.

Megan wasn't his. Even if they had been married, he held no physical claim over her. She didn't bear a stamp that said she was The Property of Darius Folsom.

But he had believed he was in possession of her heart.

He remembered the devastated shadow in her eyes last night. She probably did love him. But not as much as he loved her.

He'd never in a million years think about being unfaithful to her, physically or otherwise.

Of course, it was easy to say that when the only place he'd be was in the remote mountains of Afghanistan with nothing but other Marines and goats as company.

He rubbed the back of his neck and then reached

automatically for his side pocket where the pain medication he'd finally started taking was.

He caught himself.

"We need to talk," Jason said.

His ex-friend had come up beside him while he wasn't looking.

"We have nothing to say to each other."

Jason sighed heavily and put his hands on his hips. "Hey, the last time I checked we held equal interest in this company."

"Not for long."

Jason squinted at him. "How do you mean?"

"It means we'll never have to worry about confronting that issue again."

With that, he left the room, deciding to leave any necessary communicating to Linc.

JASON WANTED TO HIT something as he watched Dari walk away from him. His head still pounded from last night's overindulgence. But for a short time, the alcohol helped him forget what he'd done.

Shit.

While the scene with Dari in his motel bathroom was a bit blurry, he was pretty clear on the fact he'd been the one to tell his best friend he'd had sex with his girlfriend.

He cursed himself inwardly. He'd been so certain Megan had told him. Hadn't she said she was going to do as much? Why hadn't she?

And why had he opened his big mouth?

"Ready?"

He looked to see Linc at his side.

"Yeah. Let's get this over with. Who else is coming?"

A couple of the team members stepped up.

Through Linc's contacts at the FBI, they'd learned not only the exact place where McCain had met the responding officers, but the location where he'd placed the call to the sheriff's office declaring discovery within fifty yards. It was still a lot of ground to cover, and there was no guarantee McCain had made the call from the exact point he'd found her, but they were going to go out and see what they could scare up nonetheless.

Jason led the way, ignoring the pounding of his head and the knot in his gut, focusing his energy on the day that lay ahead.

MEGAN WASN'T ENTIRELY certain what she was looking for. Perhaps satisfying closure in her life where there was so little of it to be found in other areas. But rather than wrap things up in the Finley search, she instead redirected her efforts into what had truly happened.

The story was that Finley had come across a small dog on the loose and had gone after him into the forest. She'd ridden her bike as far as she could, then abandoned it and continued on foot. Darkness had fallen, but she'd continued the chase until she could no longer hear the dog. Then she'd realized she was lost.

As for McCain, he was saying that he'd been concerned and restless after the church service, upset that the search had been abandoned for the day due to rain. So he'd taken a backpack and headed off on his own, calling for Finley as he went. Yes, he'd been afraid of getting lost himself, but he'd had GPS to guide him and a cell phone.

He was an hour inside when she finally called back to him.

He'd fed her and called the sheriff, but rather than waiting for the authorities to arrive, he'd carried Finley out of the forest himself, leaving the exact whereabouts of where she'd been a mystery.

All told, everyone was just happy she'd been found alive.

Including Megan.

But she had one or two unanswered questions she'd like to ask.

Thankfully, the family was so happy, they readily invited her to stop by for some coffee. Megan had been surprised, pleasantly so, considering they had triple the media camped out on their doorstep. But since it had been Lazarus that had found the bike, and the location of the bike had led to finding Finley, she easily gained access since she was the one they associated with the company.

Megan navigated her way through the throng of press blocking the Szymanskis' sidewalk, waving away microphones and cell phones and the questions that went along with them.

One of them recognized her.

"Miss McGowan! Miss McGowan! Tell me how you feel about your company's discovery of little Finley's bike leading to her safe return home."

That, she couldn't ignore. She paused slightly and said, "Everyone at Lazarus Security is very happy that Finley Szymanski is finally home where she belongs."

With that, she pushed her way through to the front door and was immediately led inside.

It was the grandmother who greeted her, hugging her as if she were family. The warm affection made her feel a little awkward, especially considering the reason she was there. But she returned the gesture and smiled when the older woman drew back.

"Dorma is upstairs giving Finley a bath now. She must have had at least ten since she got home. It's like she can't get clean enough."

"I think I'd feel the same if I were caught outside for that long."

She was invited into the kitchen where the other woman poured her a fresh cup of coffee and then peeled back foil on at least five different cakes neighbors and families had dropped off. Megan declined, but Finley's grandmother served up a piece of lemon coffee cake just the same then sat down opposite her with her own slice.

"How is Finley all told?" Megan asked carefully.

"Happy to be home."

"Of course."

"She was afraid she'd never get back."

"And the dog?"

"Dog? Oh, yeah. The dog." The woman laughed quietly. "Never found him again."

"Did she know the dog? Maybe it belonged to a neighbor?"

The grandmother blinked. "I'm not sure. I don't think so. She said it was like one of those Paris Hilton dogs. A Chihuahua, I guess. No one we know has one."

Megan made a note to check newspapers and online resources for any ads placed for missing dogs. Also, a call to the pound wouldn't be a bad idea.

"Has Finley said anything that the news or the sheriff's press conference hasn't covered already?"

The grandmother shifted uncomfortably. "Do you know something you're not telling me?"

"What do you mean?"

"Well, she was lost and now she's been found. She's home…"

"Yes. And I'm happy for that."

"You make it sound like there was a crime involved."

Unfortunately, she was afraid there might be. "No, no. Just covering all the bases, that's all," Megan said in what she hoped was a reassuring tone. "You know how the media can be. If there's one question left unanswered, they'll be sure to come up with their own."

"Oh my God, don't I know it…"

Then she went into almost every detail of what happened, everything Finley had said, from the moment they met the authorities at the discovery site. Or, rather, the edge of the forest, where she'd been discovered.

Unfortunately, none of it was really anything Megan could use. From what she understood, all Finley's grandmother kept talking about was the moment of discovery. About eating animal crackers and drinking the juice McCain had given her. Of his carrying her. Of the little dog that had gotten lost just like she had.

There were other questions Megan would like to have asked, but she didn't get a chance as Finley came bounding into the kitchen in her pink pj's, her damp hair combed back, a smile the size of all of Florida on her young, pretty face.

"Snack time, Mimi!"

The grandmother laughed. "Oh, and she can't seem to get enough to eat, either."

Megan could only imagine.

18

JASON SAT AT THE BAR, draining the last of the beer in his bottle. He waved the empty at the tender and then put it down, dragging the back of his wrist across his mouth.

He'd been in the place for the past hour and couldn't seem to quench his thirst. A mission the tender didn't seem to be in any hurry to assist him with.

"Hey," Dominic, one of the last remaining team members, said as he took the stool next to him.

Linc had been with him earlier, then gave him a silent salute before leaving a short time ago after only one beer.

Some company he'd been. Especially considering their visit to his FBI buddies and an exhaustive trek through the forest hadn't yielded anything more than a headache and tired muscles. Not that he'd expected otherwise, but he'd hoped to glean more than they had.

For all intents and purposes, Finley's discovery had happened exactly the way McCain represented. There was no reason for them to suspect differently.

Still, he'd feel a hell of a lot better if he could find the area where the girl said she'd stayed for the duration, never moving more than ten feet as she waited for someone to come for her.

"So, is it true?" Dominic asked.

"Tender?" Jason called out, holding up his empty bottle. "When you get a minute." He turned his attention to the kid next to him. "Is what true?"

He really wasn't up for babysitting one of the younger team members. He'd prefer to be alone, if it was all the same to everyone else. Or with Linc. Which was pretty damn close to being alone.

"Did you and the lady boss…" the kid made like he was pulling something close to his hips "…you know, knock boots?"

Jason stared at him, his every muscle tensing dangerously. The tender finally came and exchanged his empty for a full. He pulled it close, nearly draining it in one swig.

Had Linc said something? He dismissed the thought the instant it entered his head. Linc didn't speak unless it was absolutely necessary, and even then, he barely said anything at all.

He looked back at the kid.

"Hey, I'm not saying anything everyone else isn't already talking about," he said, holding up his hands. "I mean, you disappeared into her room every night. And now you, her and her old man aren't speaking."

Her old man.

He grimaced at that. The kid was new enough to the team he wasn't familiar with Dari and his connection to the company.

He also wouldn't know that Megan and Dari were a longtime couple.

Jason forced himself to push his bottle slightly away. His head already felt as if it was stuffed with cotton. "You know what they say about loose lips, kid."

"Yeah, they sink ships. Only we aren't on a ship."

No, but Jason felt very close to drowning him anyway.

He glanced around the room. A couple other team members waiting for morning and their transport out were there and openly watching him.

Damn. When had a simple roll in the hay become so damn complicated?

The waitress sidled up to stand between him and Dominic, making it obvious she was ignoring him and catering to the kid as she placed her orders with the tender.

Jason cursed under his breath. Why hadn't he just bedded the woman instead of holding on to some stupid latent desire for his best friend's girl? Even now, he could be hip deep into some sweet flesh instead of at the bar drowning his sorrows, mourning the loss of his best friend.

"So how was it?"

The kid didn't know when to shut up, did he?

"Bet she was good. She looks like she'd be majorly hot between the sheets—"

Jason wasn't sure what happened next…but he was pretty sure it involved his fist and sinking the kid's proverbial ship.

THE CHIRP OF HER CELL phone woke Megan from a dead sleep. She blindly reached for it, her heart racing.

"Hello?" she said before pressing the right button. "Hello?" she said again.

She listened for a moment, then slowly pushed herself up into a sitting position and reached for the lamp switch. "Say that again, please?"

She disconnected and then sat for long minutes listening to nothing but the hum of the air conditioner and the thud of her own heart.

Damn.

Forcing herself out of bed, she climbed into her jeans, grabbed a T-shirt, then headed for the door barefoot. Before she knew it, she was pushing her tangled hair from her face and knocking on Linc's door. She wasn't surprised when it opened to reveal a fully dressed and alert Linc.

"Hey," she said. "Is…"

She didn't have to finish the question. Dari

was already next to Linc, taking his place in the doorway.

"What is it?" he asked, appearing as disoriented as she felt.

Still, the immediate concern on his handsome face, and the way he leaped when he heard her at the door, made her pulse jump.

So much so, she regretted saying what she was about to.

"It's Savage," she said. "He got into a barroom brawl and is in the county lockup."

The softness on his face vanished, replaced by hardness. "Why are you telling me this?"

"He tried calling you but you didn't pick up."

He scrubbed his hand over his face and then back over his closely cropped hair.

"He's in the next county. Do you have any sway with the sheriff to act as intermediary?"

"Why in the hell would I want to do that? Maybe he should just cool his heels behind bars. He got into the fight. He should pay the consequences."

"The altercation was with Dominic Falzone."

His brows rose. "Damn."

"Tell me about it."

They stood there silently for long moments, neither of them saying anything, nor appearing to know what to do at all.

Should she offer to go with him? As much as she wanted to, she didn't think it a good idea. Whatever was going on between the two men needed to be sorted out between the two men.

As for her and Dari…

Her stomach clenched.

Well, she was growing increasingly fearful that there was no her and Dari. Not anymore.

"I'll take care of it."

She nodded and then sucked her bottom lip between her teeth.

"Good night."

"Oh. Yeah. Good night."

The door closed softly in her face.

Megan tried to blink back tears, but found them streaming down her cheeks instead. She turned and hurried to her room where she could let them roll unchecked.

JASON'S HEAD POUNDED, as much from the drink as from the stool he'd taken to the back of it. What had started as a simple fist throwing had quickly escalated into an outright brawl with everyone with a gripe in the bar joining in the melee.

He wasn't amused he was the only one pulled in.

Just when he thought things couldn't possibly get any worse, they had.

He heard the jangling of keys. He turned his head where he lay across a small, metal bunk and watched a deputy approach the bars.

"Better get up, Savage. Seems you have some friends in high places."

Jason flipped him off.

"Nice. I love you, too." The man opened the bars.

Jason pushed up from the bunk, swaying slightly before regaining his balance and stepping through the open door.

A minute later he faced the one responsible for springing him: Dari. The last person on earth he would have expected.

They stood staring at each other.

"I need you to sign here for your personal effects," the deputy said, shoving an oversize Ziploc bag holding a wallet and change in his direction along with a form.

Jason did as asked and then tilted his things from the bag. When he turned around, Dari was gone.

He hurried out the door.

"Hey!" he called out to where Dari was heading for one of the rented SUVs.

Dari stopped but didn't turn.

Jason advanced on him.

It was still dark, but dawn's bruised fingers were beginning to grip the sky to the east, telling him the morning wasn't far off. The air was thick and heavy and still, a harbinger for another hot, stormy day.

"Are you ever planning to talk to me about this?"

He caught the way Dari clenched and unclenched his fists.

"You're not really going to throw away years of friendship because of one stupid mistake, are you?"

Dari swung toward him. "Now it's a mistake? The other night it was just sex."

Jason's frown went bone deep. "It was just sex. The mistake part enters in where you're concerned."

He crossed his arms, apparently waiting.

Jason glanced at the SUV and then rubbed the top of his head. "Look, why don't we talk about this over breakfast. I've got a splitting headache and could really use a cup of coffee."

Dari didn't budge.

"Fine. You want to have this out here, we'll have this out here then."

Still nothing.

"Look, I never intended for you to find out, man…"

Dari looked dangerously like he must have last night when the kid refused to shut up.

Hell.

"Scratch that. Hey, I know nothing I could ever say could make this any better for you. What happened between Megan and I had nothing to do with love…"

Dari's hand slammed against his chest so quickly Jason didn't know what hit him until he was flat against the side of the SUV. "It had everything to do with love—my love for her."

Jason stayed still, not daring to contradict him. "And her love for you?" he asked.

Dari released him.

"She does love you, you know."

"I know." Dari moved toward the driver's side of the SUV.

"So what's the problem then?"

His friend turned on him and jabbed a finger in his direction. "The problem is that I learned the hard way that I can't trust the two most important people in my life."

"Bullshit. You can trust both of us with your life."

"But not my heart."

Jason put his hands on his hips. "Oh, give me a break. You sound like a fifteen-year-old girl with a crush."

"Fuck you, Savage."

"Excuse me, but I think that's how this whole thing got started to begin with."

He didn't see the fist coming until it connected with his right brow. He stumbled back a couple of steps and then lifted his hand to find blood trickling from a gash.

"I probably deserve that."

"You deserve much more."

He nodded. "You're right." He sighed. "Look, I've never been in love. Not like you and Meg. I pretend to understand what you're going through, but the truth is

I don't have a clue. If you tell me your heart is aching, I'm likely to tell you to buy antacids."

"Which is why I can't talk to you. Now or ever."

Darius climbed into the SUV, started it and began pulling away, forcing Jason to step back before he got sideswiped.

He kicked at the gravel and cursed a blue streak, damning himself and his oversexed libido to hell and back.

19

Two days later, Megan retraced her steps from the firing range at the Lazarus compound back in Colorado Springs. Would there come a time when her feet would feel lighter? When she could lift her head without major effort? When her heart didn't feel like a lump of pulsing, aching lead in her chest?

She knew that time would heal everything. But right then, it didn't feel that way.

As far as she could tell, Dari had yet to return home from Florida. Or at least, he hadn't returned to Colorado or his apartment.

She, on the other hand, was aware of every tick of the clock since her return. She kept busy with Lazarus, jumping right back in where she left off, then spent her nights reviewing the Finley case, even though it was officially closed and the national news media had stopped airing coverage.

She glanced over at where Jason had just knocked a recruit's boot with one of his to get him to widen his shooting stance, and then raised the guy's hold. He didn't appear to be doing much better than she was. Not that they'd talked about it. She didn't think it a good idea to be caught talking to him for any extended period in case Dari did plan to return. It was something she barely dared hope for, but did nonetheless.

It was the end of another long day, with another long night yawning in front of her like a fathomless hole. She was lucky if she remembered to eat and she never quite remembered how she made it from the compound to home, although she apparently managed it safely.

She opened the compound door, cleaned and stored the weapon she'd used for target practice and then ran straight into Jason who apparently had the same idea.

"Sorry," he said quietly, avoiding her gaze.

She took a deep breath and released it. "This is ridiculous. How long are we going to keep avoiding each other?"

He met her gaze. "I figured until the end of the millennium at least."

That inspired a small smile. "That's a pretty long time."

"Tell me about it."

Conversation lagged and a couple of recruits came in and made their way around where they stood. Megan watched them, thinking she should move on before causing any more unwanted gossip.

Jason's voice stopped her. "You know, I don't think I ever told you, you know…"

His words drifted off.

The hesitation was so unlike Jason, Megan couldn't help wondering what he'd gone through over the past week since Dari's return from overseas. She'd been so consumed with her own drama she hadn't stopped to consider his.

Perhaps in some way she had blamed him. Had he not made that suggestion that night…well, they would never have slept together.

But that was a cop out. She went into it knowing full well what she was doing.

And despite everything that had transpired in the interim, it had been exactly what she'd needed at the time.

"I'm sorry," he said finally.

Megan raised her brows, fairly certain she was hearing things. "Pass that by me again?"

He grimaced. "Have you ever considered the reason guys don't apologize often is because you girls make it so damn tough?"

She raised a hand. "No, no. I'm not asking you to repeat yourself for any other reason than I can't figure out what you're sorry for."

He shifted on his feet.

To say the atmosphere between them had been stressed since Dari's return was a considerable understatement. But they'd both accepted responsibility for their actions. And they both were now paying the price.

"What isn't there to be sorry for?" Jason asked. "From making that stupid-ass suggestion, to telling Dari about it and everything in between, I think there's a whole lot of apologizing to be done. On my part."

She was speechless.

"That's got to be the dumbest thing I've ever heard," she said.

They stood looking at each other for a long time.

Jason had always been the one who knew his own mind. Who made instinctive decisions and stuck to them, without hesitation. It was one of the qualities that had made him so effective on the battlefield... and successful as a business partner.

Why was he backing away from that now?

Megan ultimately shook her head. "Apology not accepted."

She turned to walk away and he lightly grasped her arm.

"I've already lost one goddamn friend over this. I don't want to lose another."

She smiled. "You're not. Losing a second friend, that is. I don't accept your apology because you have nothing to be sorry for."

He stared at her as if unsure she was telling the truth.

"Seriously," she added.

"So what you're telling me is that this is the first time I've apologized to a woman in my life, and there was no reason to…"

"Oh, that can't possibly be true," she said. Then she looked at him closer. "Was that really the first time you've apologized to a woman?"

His grimace told her it was.

"Wow."

"Tell me about it."

"Well, I suppose that's progress…"

"Yeah, but progress toward what?"

She laid a hand on his shoulder. "Toward becoming a man."

He snorted and she laughed, something that felt good if only because it seemed so long since she'd done it.

MEGAN SAT CROSS-LEGGED on her bed much later that night, half-eaten egg foo yong in a carton at her left knee, her folder on the Finley case at her right. The television ran a DVD of different video segments the girls at the office had put together for her on Finley's recovery. They'd even included some portions from while she was missing, mostly snippets where Lazarus personnel were speaking.

But just then, she paid attention to none of it. She had her cell phone in her hands, checking for messages. There were none. Same with texts.

Biting her bottom lip, she scrolled through her address book until she came to Dari's name, then pulled it up onto the screen. Her thumb hovered over the call button…where it stayed for long moments before she canceled the request and tossed the cell to the bed with the rest of the items surrounding her.

Today's exchange with Jason had proved a salve of sorts, which she hadn't expected. She hadn't been aware of the rift that existed there until he offered up his awkward apology. Not that they'd ever been the best friends he and Dari were, but there had been friendship. And they'd lost that in the wake of the disaster last week.

While they were a ways away from becoming close buds, it was nice to be able to call him a friend again.

She only wished other areas of her life could be as easily repaired.

She glanced at the television to find a shot of little Finley being carried from the sheriff's office by her grandfather, the blanket over her head to protect her from the cameras sliding off a bit. Megan reached for the remote and turned up the volume, although there was nothing to be heard over the cacophony of reporters' questions.

The blanket slipped farther…

The cell phone rang. In her hurry to answer, she toppled the take-out carton onto the floor.

"Hello?"

"Meggie?"

Her dad.

The butterflies in her stomach slowed the hopeful flapping of their wings. Not Dari.

"Hi, Dad," she said, picking up the remote and muting the television volume. "How are you?"

"Fine. I'm fine. And you?"

"Fine."

Silence. Which was pretty much the hallmark of the majority of their conversations over the years. She had become so accustomed to the routine, she'd never considered she had the power to change it.

Until now.

"Dad, what are you doing right now?"

It was seven-thirty on a weeknight. She knew he was probably settled in for *Jeopardy!* and then would follow that with either a novel or biography before retiring at ten.

"Pardon me?" He sounded surprised.

"I was thinking I could bring over a pint of your favorite butter-pecan ice cream and we could have a visit."

Silence. But this time it wasn't because neither of them had anything to say.

She'd never dared make such a suggestion before. Upset the routine. She wasn't really sure why. But she was determined it was long past time that both of them began living outside their regimented lives.

"Well, yes. I'd like that," he said, warmth in his voice. "I'd like that a lot…"

20

DARI ENTERED HIS Colorado Springs apartment feeling as if he wore lead shoes rather than his regular military-issue boots. The place was stuffy. Not surprising, since he hadn't been there in over four months. He knew Megan had aired it out on a regular basis while he was away, but now…

As he adjusted the thermostat to a lower temperature, he caught a glimpse of a note on the counter next to the refrigerator. He read it where it sat:

> *I left your key by the door and removed my personal belongings. There's condensed milk and cereal in the cupboard along with a few other nonperishables. Didn't know when or if you'd be back.*
> *Love,*
> *Megan.*

He stared at the note for long moments, waiting for his heart to unclench. Then he picked it up, causing something to clink underneath. His eyes focused on the engagement ring he'd given her. She had returned it as casually as his house key.

He picked the ring up, staring at it, then slid it up and down his pinkie finger several times before shoving it into his pants pocket.

He'd stayed on in Florida for a couple of extra days, hoping the time would help make his return home easier. It hadn't. If anything, it seemed to worsen it. The weight of Megan's absence throbbed as badly as his injured leg.

He put the note down on the counter and checked the cupboards. She'd bought far more than her note indicated. The evidence of her regular generosity despite what had happened between them made the ache more acute.

He collected the extra key from where she'd left it near the door, rubbing it between his thumb and fingers until the metal grew warm to the touch. Then he put it on his key ring next to the other.

Damn. Why did he feel guilty when he was the one who had been wronged?

That was a sensation he hadn't expected to experience. It emerged the night she left Florida, and seemed to feed on the lengthening gap growing between them ever since.

He caught himself rubbing his leg above his knee. In the wake of Jason's admission, he hadn't given a great deal of thought to his injury, and had begun to fear it had become infected. But a visit to a Florida

VA hospital had shown it was healing nicely, although probably not as quickly as it could. He'd need to rest more for that to happen.

Rest. A foreign word to him.

He hefted his duffel and tossed it to the corner where it would stay untouched unless he needed something. He already had a call into command requesting administrative duty in Afghanistan until he could go full active. He didn't expect to hear immediately, but was hoping word would come down soon. The faster he was out of here, the better.

His cell vibrated in his pocket. He pulled it out even as he stepped toward the kitchen sink and turned on the cold water full blast.

Jason.

He put the phone back in his pocket, ignoring the call along with the others his onetime friend had made over the past few days. He leaned against the sink and splashed water over his face several times, glad for the cold and its clarifying effects. He shut off the faucet.

A knock at the door.

Water dripping from his chin, he glanced in that direction. No one knew he was coming back. Even his parents thought he was still in Florida. A neighbor, maybe? The manager delivering the mail he'd held?

He pulled the door open to find Jason standing there, his cell phone to his ear, its ringing coinciding with the incessant vibrating in his pocket.

Jason closed the cell and dropped it to his side.

"Hey," he said.

Dari wiped the water from his face. "Hey."

He turned from the door and went for the kitchen towel hanging next to the sink, mopping the remainder of water from his chin and hands.

"You didn't pick up my call."

"Yeah, well, had I known it was you at the door, I wouldn't have answered that, either." Dari turned toward him. "I just got here. How did you know I'd be home?"

Jason stepped inside and closed the door behind him. "Have you really so quickly forgotten the nature of the business we opened together?"

Dari stared at him.

"I knew the instant you got on that plane and the minute it arrived. I would have picked you up there, but I was afraid you might turn around and catch the next flight out."

"Your fear would have been justified." Dari wadded the towel up in his hands. "What in the hell do you want?"

"What in the hell do you think I want?"

"I wouldn't have asked if I had any idea what you're doing here."

"We need to talk."

"I already told you—"

"Christ, who knew you were the type to haul a boulder to hell and back without taking a breather?"

"Who? You. At least you should have had you

half been paying attention. Oh, wait. You hadn't. You were too busy trying to back my girlfriend into bed."

"Low blow."

Dari knew it was. But, damn it, he was entitled to make a couple of jabs below the belt.

"That's not how it went down and you know it."

"Do I? Because I'm having an awfully hard time believing otherwise."

"Well, then, maybe you should step back and take another look."

Dari threw the towel toward the kitchen counter with so much force it took out a glass in the drainer. The sound of breaking glass filled the room. Not that he heard it over the roar in his ears. "I have taken another look. I've stared at the goddamn thing from every angle, and it still makes zero sense to me."

Jason advanced on him. Only this time, he was clear-eyed and determined, whereas in Florida, he'd been suffering a hangover. "Will you climb down off the cross already? We need the freakin' wood."

Dari wanted to hit him so badly his knuckles itched.

"What happened was unfortunate. It wasn't a purposeful crime against you or anyone else." His onetime friend seemed to have a death wish. "God, are you so stupid you can't see how much the woman loves you?"

Dari opened his mouth to respond.

"I know what happened was wrong. Hell, we

all do. But we can't take it back. But we *can* move forward."

He paced a short ways away and then back again.

"When you first met Megan, I remember being jealous. Not of you. I was jealous of her. Because she took a big chunk of your time away from me."

"Right."

Jason held up his hand. "Shut up until I'm done, will you?"

Dari began to step forward then stopped.

"I've watched you and Megan for the past two and a half years. Hell, until I saw the two of you together, I'd always thought love was a word. Oh, lust, passion, sex, I knew all those well. But love? Completely foreign."

Then why did you sleep with her? The words were on the tip of Dari's tongue; exactly where they stayed.

"I've never regretted anything else in my life, man," Jason said quietly. "Not like I regret coming between the two of you."

Sincerity ran in his words. Dari was incapable of a worthy response. So he made none.

"What I'm trying to say is…what in the hell are you doing? She loves you, Dar. And you obviously love her…"

His words trailed off, the territory uncharted to him.

"I asked her to marry me." Dari wasn't sure why he'd offered up that bit of humiliating info.

He flinched at the memory, dropping to one knee and offering his soul up along with the heart he'd lost to her long ago.

Remembering her tears—her gentle refusal that he'd believed was fear but now knew was guilt—felt like razor wire twisting through his gut.

"Before or after?" Jason asked.

"Before."

"Oh, hell…"

"Do you really think I would have done it after?"

Jason stared at him. "I think if you were smart, it's exactly what you'd do."

Dari went to the door and opened it wide. "Get out."

Jason shook his head. "Fine. I'll go." He walked until he was parallel to him, but Dari refused to meet his gaze. "But it's only for now. I'm not going to give up, man. You may have given up on me, on Megan. But I'm not going to. Not now. Not ever."

He walked through the door.

Dari slammed it so forcefully it nearly rattled off the hinges.

MEGAN LAY ACROSS HER BED, thinking about the past hour spent with her dad. It could have been the unexpected nature of her visit, or the ice cream, but she'd enjoyed time with him and was certain he'd felt the same.

Why hadn't she thought of doing something like that before? Why had they limited their contact to weekly phone calls and biweekly lunches?

She recognized part of the reason was she found it all too easy to focus on the negatives of their relationship rather than the positives. Yes, her dad was traditional. And he would have liked her to be more like her ultrafeminine mother. But that didn't mean he didn't love her the way she was. In fact, she was coming to see that their similarities might allow for a closer connection than they'd have had if things had turned out the way he wanted. They had a lot in common. But at the same time, she was still—and always would be—his little girl.

And she also saw that being feminine didn't have to mean being weak.

She logged onto her laptop even as she switched on the television and the DVD she'd been watching earlier. She had a new email message. She opened it up, smiling when she saw it was from Dorothy.

I know this may sound odd, but I miss you! the young woman began.

Megan missed her, as well. She'd never really had any female friends outside the military. But Dorothy and her little girl had touched a spot within her she hadn't known existed. And that spot grew exponentially each time she thought of them both.

Daisy says she misses you, too. I've included a photo of her I took earlier today.

Megan scrolled down. There was little Daisy wearing one of her pretty dresses, her hands on the hem as if about to lift it and flash her undies.

She laughed...until she spotted something else.

There was a scarf tied around her tiny neck.

A chill scurried up her spine. She scrolled back up to the message, but no mention was made of the presence of the scarf. She scrambled for the remote, going back to the footage of when Finley was being carried out of the sheriff's office, the blanket protecting her from camera view shifting, until...a scarf was revealed...

21

THE HOUSE ALWAYS seemed overly bright, as if the owner was trying to eradicate all darkness. As a result, there was no color, only a sterile whiteness that was nearly blinding.

Dari was accustomed to this. His mother had always decorated in a like manner. White on white on white. Oh, she always knew the different shades of white, but to him it had always been white.

And he'd always been overly cautious of smudging it.

"Come in, come in!" his father said, enthusiastically patting him on the back. "Let's go into the kitchen. I've been dying for an excuse to try out my new coffee blend on a willing victim."

"What about Mother?"

"She doesn't drink coffee. You know that."

No, his mother always drank tea. In a dainty cup.

"Is she home?"

"No, no. Tonight's her monthly women's-group meeting. She won't be back for an hour or so."

Dari reflexively relaxed.

He sat down at a stool next to the kitchen island, watching as his father readied the high-end coffee-maker and then turned around to face him.

"I didn't think we'd see you before you shipped out again."

Dari frowned. "I didn't think you would either."

"You worked that missing-girl case in Florida?"

"Somewhat." If you could call what he did work-ing. At any rate, it certainly wasn't going to be what he remembered about the experience.

"And Megan? How is she? Would have been nice to see her as well."

A vise tightened around Dari's chest. "She couldn't make it."

He couldn't quite bring himself to tell his father that he and Megan were no longer together. If only because he'd have to explain why. And he couldn't do that with any degree of objectivity. Not yet. Although he understood at some point, he'd have to.

"So, you're going back to Afghanistan."

"Actually, they're sending me to a desk job in Iraq first. You know, until I heal."

He'd been adamant about accepting any post, get-ting out of the country as soon as he possibly could. He understood that his injury needed to heal. But right now, it was imperative that his broken heart started healing, too. And he had to be far, far away in order to do that.

The coffee finished brewing and his father poured two cups, handing him one. He knew better than to request sugar or cream; his father's concoctions were meant to be tried black.

Dari sipped. Never having been a coffee connoisseur, he couldn't tell the difference between this or any other cup of coffee, but he made the required sounds of approval.

"Good, huh? Can you taste the hazelnut?"

"Is that what it is?" He nodded. "I like it."

His father looked pleased and in the end, that's all that mattered.

Then again, his father always somehow managed to make the best out of a situation. Dari knew that from experience. As a kid he'd watched his dad suffer through his mom's many depressions and "episodes," as other family members on both sides liked to refer to them. The only thing holding them all together was Dad, sometimes simply by sheer force of will.

"Dad? May I ask you something?"

He looked surprised. "Sure, Darius. You don't have to request permission."

Dari tried for a smile, but couldn't quite swing it. "How could you stay with Mom after she was unfaithful to you?"

Derek Folsom blinked at him, apparently incapable of words.

"I'm sorry to just put it out there like that…"

His father appeared to struggle with his response. "No, no. I, um, find with items of that nature, it's always best to just, um, put it right out there." He laughed without humor. "Actually, there really isn't any other way, is there?"

Dari shifted on his stool. "I guess what I'm trying to say is…you're so strong in every other area of your life. You retired from the military, started your own business and became very successful. You've won nearly every business and civic award out there…"

His father frowned into his coffee. Dari wasn't big on having ruined his special blend for him.

"And yet you allowed a woman to turn you into a cuckold."

Derek flinched and then sat quietly for long moments. Dari considered retracting the question. Apologizing for having posed it. But he needed the answer. Needed to apply it to his own situation. Perhaps to verify he was doing the right thing.

"Is that what you think?" Derek asked, squinting at him. "That your mother did me wrong?"

"Is there really any other way to see it?"

His father leaned back. "Yes. Yes, there is. You can see the truth."

"I know the truth. I lived it. Remember?"

"No, son," he said quietly. "You know what other family members thought they knew."

Silence.

Then finally Dari prompted, "I'm listening."

"I know you are. It's just I'm having a hard time coming up with the words to explain it to you."

He couldn't possibly imagine anything his father could tell him would alter his perception of the situation. Was his dad still covering for his mother? He suspected he was.

"You see, back when we first met, your mother and I...I was dating someone else..."

Dari raised his brows. This went back that far?

"I loved Patricia. And she loved me. But we had a volatile relationship—one month on, two months off. That sort of thing..." He trailed off and an almost wistful expression took hold of his face. One that made him look twenty years younger. "Then I met your mom..."

Dari's hands tightened on his coffee cup.

"She was everything a woman was supposed to be and I fell in love with her instantly."

He couldn't quite see where this was leading.

"The problem was, I never fell out of love with Patricia. In fact, I never fell out of love with her, period."

Dari stared at him. "Are you saying... You can't possibly mean..."

"Yes. Over the years I continued to see Patricia. Even as your mom and I dated, married, had you..."

Dari winced. "Mom knew?"

"On occasion, yes. Mostly I protected her from it."

He couldn't have been surprised more had his

dad told him he wasn't his biological son. "Are you serious?"

"Unfortunately, yes. I'm completely serious."

Dari tried to digest what he'd been told. His father had been in love with another woman for the entire length of his relationship with his mother. "So that's why Mom…"

His father nodded. Then he blew out a long breath, looking more his age again. "I tried. I really did. You know, to stay loyal to your mother."

"Do you love Patricia more?"

"What? No." He sat back. "You see, I loved them both."

"You say that as in past tense."

He nodded. "Yes. You see, I lost Patricia to breast cancer four years ago."

Dari's head spun from the shock of it all.

"Funny thing is, your mother was the strongest out of all of us. She actually took her in here. You were still serving back then. All you knew was that your mom had a friend staying…"

Dari remembered the conversations with his mother. He'd had no cause to think circumstances were any different than what she represented.

"Patricia and I never had children. Your mom and I were lucky to have had you. I…I, um, took you to see Patricia a couple of times when you were younger. Not that you'd remember. But I was afraid Patricia would grow attached and…well, that wasn't a good idea."

"Why?" Dari asked. "Why did you do it?"

"Love," his father said simply.

Dari was dumbfounded.

"You see, son, there are certain things you come to learn in life. One of them is, 'Love isn't about who you can live with, it's about who you can't live without.' It so happened that I had two beautiful women that fit that description."

"I don't quite know what to say..."

All these years he'd blamed his mother. He'd thought her the unfaithful one. And, yes, while she'd gone outside the marriage, he thought he somewhat understood why she had now.

"Trust me, if I could go back and do everything differently..." He drew a deep breath. "Then again, no. I wouldn't change a thing. I loved loving both your mother and Patricia. But I do know it wasn't fair to either of them. Patricia was never able to find love with anyone else. And your mother...well, we both know all too well what happened there." He swallowed hard, the sound loud in the quiet room. "Thankfully she's been able to find a patch of peace now that Patricia's gone. And I think she also reached an understanding of sorts while she cared for her. Still, there's not a day that goes by I don't regret hurting them both."

In Dari's eyes, his father had always been the wronged one. Not the one doing wrong.

"Do you love Megan?" his father asked.

Dari drew back.

"Stupid question. I know you love her. Well, then, let me give you this bit of advice, son. You know, if I'm still entitled to do so."

He wasn't sure who was entitled to what just then, but Dari gestured for his dad to continue.

"If you love her, hang on to her. Don't let go and go on to love someone else. Because if it's one lesson I learned it's that love…true love…it doesn't stop because you will it to. It continues to go on and on."

Dari's heart contracted in his chest at the thought that he'd always feel this pain. This total inability to feel anything else. "But isn't it possible for that love to be destroyed?"

His father shook his head. "No. Not permanently. Oh, you may believe it's possible. You can do everything within your power to make it so. But I learned the hard way that unconditional love is…well, truly unconditional."

Dari's cell phone rang. At first he didn't register it. Then he shook his head as if to clear it and slid the device out of his pocket.

Lazarus.

A text followed when he didn't answer.

Urgent was all it said.

After a couple more minutes of seeking understanding, but only managing to come away with more questions, he thanked his dad for the coffee—and for the truth—then bid him goodbye. Silently, he made a vow to seek out his mother more. Having been through what he had with Megan, he couldn't imagine what it must have been like for her to know his father had loved another woman. It must have nearly driven her insane.

In fact, at times, it had.

And his own narrow-minded understanding of the truth couldn't have helped any.

Why had she never told him?

Perhaps because she'd protected him.

Protected him when he'd condemned her.

Dari's heart hurt even harder....

MEGAN PACED THE LENGTH of Lazarus's conference room, checking to make sure the DVD was cued to the right place before switching the television off and glancing at her watch for the time, anxious for everyone to show. She'd contacted the front office from home and had messages sent out to the main members of the Finley team, requesting their urgent presence.

She'd included Dari. Not that she expected him to come.

Oh, she knew he was back in town. You couldn't work at a place that specialized in matters of location and security and not know everything going on, no matter how much you might not want to know those things.

It was nearing midnight. A late hour, to be sure, but this couldn't sit until morning. And neither could she.

Jason was the first to arrive, followed by Linc.

They both poured themselves coffee from the pot in the corner, despite the late hour. After five minutes, she was reasonably sure Dari wouldn't be coming.

"So, let's begin, shall we?" she said, switching on the television.

To her surprise, Dari walked into the room.

Her heart pitched to her feet and then boomeranged back up to lodge in her throat.

She hadn't seen him for a couple of weeks. In some ways it felt like an eternity. In others, mere minutes ago.

He briefly met her gaze. But the emotion there in his eyes was unfamiliar to her.

Jason cleared his throat. Linc shook Dari's hand, welcoming him back.

Megan tried to concentrate on the matter at hand. "Okay. Now that we're, um, all here…"

She turned back to the TV screen where an image of Finley and her scarf was frozen.

"I know who kidnapped Finley," she said simply, looking at each of them in turn. "And I'm afraid he's already set his sights on his next victim…."

After receiving Dorothy's email earlier, and seeing the scarf, she was reminded of what McCain had said to her about Finley's favorite item being her pink scarf. So she'd checked the missing persons report— there was no mention of her wearing a scarf. Yet when she was found, there it was, tied nicely around her neck.

The same way the scarf had been wrapped around little Daisy.

She'd called Dorothy immediately and discovered that, yes, McCain had given her the gift earlier that day. Without giving anything away, she warned the woman to keep a close watch on her child.

"But the Finley girl has been interviewed extensively," Dari said. "There's no reason to believe she was kidnapped."

The sound of his voice was enough to knock her back off kilter. But the fact that he was talking to her nearly left her speechless.

She forced herself to look at everything but him as she lifted a finger. "That's the puzzling part of it all," she said. "You see, I've been going through my notes. Of what we've been able to piece together of her statement, both when she was found, and what her grandmother shared with me during my visit. She mentioned McCain finding her, and bringing her food…"

"When he found her," Jason added.

"Yes, but my theory is that he continued to do it throughout her isolation, because—"

"You think he led her out there…" Dari said.

She smiled. "No. I know he did. Because I have a solid connection between a dog coincidentally like the dog Finley followed into the woods and McCain."

22

THE INSTANT MEGAN finished explaining her theory and presenting her proof, the guys sprang into action. Linc left without saying a word, presumably to consult with his FBI friends. Jason and Dari walked out together to get on the next plane back to Florida—on a private charter if need be.

Just watching the two working together, as if nothing had ever come between them, made Megan's knees weak. She dropped into the closest chair until she could regain her bearings.

Since leaving Florida, she hadn't dared allow herself to hope things could ever be anything more than coldly cordial.

If Dari could forgive Jason…

She'd shaken the thought off and gone home. There was nothing more for her to do than keep on top of things from here. And she could do that via her cell and laptop. So there was no need to stay by herself at the compound.

It was just after two in the morning and she was wide awake sitting cross-legged in the middle of her bed, her laptop open in front of her, her cell phone at her knee. She'd received a text from Jason saying a charter had been secured. She was glad. Still, she'd have been happier had Dari sent it.

The television was on and an old creature feature played on low. She glanced at it every now and again, but didn't pay it much mind. What did capture her attention was the fact that her stomach was growling.

She hadn't taken more than a couple bites of her Chinese takeout earlier, so other than the bowl of ice cream she'd shared with her father, she hadn't had much of anything all day. Of course, a mere twenty-four hours ago that wouldn't have made any difference. She wouldn't have picked up on her body's signals at all, outside of the breathless ache that was becoming a permanent resident in her chest.

Was this a sign she was beginning the long, slow recovery process?

"No, dummy, it means you're hungry."

She sighed and rearranged the items on the bed so she could get up. She was wearing one of Dari's old T-shirts and plain white panties as she padded down the hall and into the kitchen where she indulged in a long session of refrigerator staring.

Nothing interested her.

She opened and closed drawers, moved items around and then finally began taking out sandwich fixings. She pushed from her mind that this was exactly what she and Dari used to do after a particularly hot and sweaty sack session: get up in the middle of the night for a couple of monster sandwiches…before heading back to bed again to take up where they'd left off.

In fact, they often didn't even make it back to the bed right away but instead resumed their lovemaking right here in the kitchen. She eyed the counter before slapping the deli meat down on top of it.

Everywhere she looked, she was reminded of him…of them together. If things didn't improve on that front, a change of residence might be in order—if only so she could move on with her life.

The idea slowed her movements as she took a couple of slices of whole-wheat bread from the loaf bag and put them on a plate.

"Got enough for two?"

The words caused her heart to hopscotch.

Great. Now she was imagining things. For a moment there, she could have sworn that was Dari's voice.

She should probably start looking into new apartments in the morning.

She layered roast beef on a bread slice and then turned back to the refrigerator to collect cheese, horseradish and green leaf lettuce…and then ran straight into Dari where he stood behind her…

DARI'S MOUTH WAS SO DRY he could barely swallow. Everything that had transpired over the past three weeks sped through his mind like myriad shooting stars: the exploding IED, his treatment, coming to Florida, proposing to Megan, her betrayal.

But just as quickly as it all entered, it exited, leaving him standing in front of her, a man looking at the woman he loved.

Oh, it had always been there. No matter how hurt he was. Or angry. The love his father had spoken of remained. And he sensed it always would. The question was, what was he going to do about it?

"I… You…" Megan finally blinked her big blue eyes, looking more female-sexy than Marine-capable. He'd always loved that intriguing contrast. Soft cries and killer instincts—an irresistible combo.

"How did you get in?" she finally asked.

He raised his hand where her house key was still on his ring. Whether he took it off and offered it back would be up to her.

"I thought you were going to Florida with Jason."

"He's a big boy. He can handle it himself."

She stared at him in a way that told him she probably wasn't registering half of what he said. Which was okay with him. He wasn't registering much of anything himself.

Besides, he'd much rather be doing something other than talking. His gaze trailed to her mouth, wanting to kiss her so badly he ached with the need.

"Look…" he began, trying to concentrate even as

he wondered if she'd welcome his kiss. The needy shadow on her face told him yes, but he wasn't convinced. "I…"

Words deserted him. At least any that held meaning.

"I would really like one of those famous sandwiches of yours." He smiled.

She blinked, openly confused.

Then she half nodded, half shook her head as if incapable of deciding on one or the other. "Okay. Yes. Sure."

She didn't ask him what he wanted on it. She already knew.

She turned back toward the counter. He stepped up next to her to help, his arm brushing hers, each time shooting sparks of want down to his groin.

She motioned for him to move so she could get into the drawer he blocked. He did and she removed a knife with which to cut the two, two-inch-thick sandwiches.

She handed him his, not letting go right away as she finally met his gaze again.

"Megan?" he asked after a long moment.

"Huh?"

"Are you going to let go of the plate?"

A heartbeat of a pause. "Oh!" She released it.

He stepped toward the small table with two chairs they'd bought together at a flea market and sat down. It took her slightly longer to follow suit. He watched her pass, the hem of his old T-shirt brushing the top of her toned thighs, the back pulled up slightly so her white panties and the half crescents of her nicely rounded behind tempted his tongue.

They ate in silence for a while, with him motioning for her to continue whenever she stopped and stared at him.

Finally, she slowly brushed the crumbs from her hands and got up to get a couple of beers from the fridge. The instant she sat down again, she asked, "What does this mean?"

He didn't respond as he reached across and took one of the beers she'd brought over.

"Don't get me wrong. It's great…wonderful to see you. But, well…" She squinted at him. "What does it mean?"

The question rendered him incapable of eating or drinking.

"I…"

He, what?

"Love isn't about who you can live with, it's about who you can't live without."

She stared at him harder.

Dari tried for a grin. "Something my father shared with me earlier." He closed his eyes briefly, emptying his mind of the other information his father had shared. An incredible story he had yet to digest. But not now.

"I've been doing a lot of thinking since you left Florida," he said. "Hell, I haven't been able to do anything but think…"

She looked down and he watched her pull her bottom lip between her teeth. He'd always been mesmerized by the telltale move. She was a confident woman, skilled at so many things. Yet that sign of inner vulnerability never failed to move him.

"I said some things out of hurt," he said quietly, wishing he could retract much of what he'd done over the past days. "I'm sorry for that."

She looked stunned.

Were his words really that implausible?

"Are you apologizing to me?" Her words were so quiet he nearly didn't hear her.

"Yes."

She fell silent again. Then she opened and closed her mouth several times, as if she had something to say but couldn't quite fit her tongue around it.

Dari's gaze homed in on the movement, his own mouth watering at the idea of kissing hers.

No matter how long they were together, how many times they made love, he couldn't seem to get enough of her. And he was coming to suspect he'd feel that way till his dying day.

And he'd prefer to experience his life with her than without.

"Does that mean… Is it possible…"

He waited for her to finish one of the sentences.

"Do you forgive me?"

It was his turn to look down. "Yes," he said simply, but kept the rest to himself.

He knew it would take a while for him to forget.

But one day he trusted he would. This would all be some long-ago, faded memory, a wound that had healed but left a scar behind as substantial as the one on his leg. But just as he would push forward and not let his physical injuries impede his progress, he didn't intend to let this emotional one keep him down.

"I love you, Megan. It's as simple and as complicated as that. And if you still love me..."

He sat looking at her for long moments. And then, as if by mutual consent, they pushed the dishes and bottles in front of them aside and reached for each other. He wasn't happy until he'd dragged her across the table and had her legs wrapped around his hips.

She kissed him over and over again, running her fingers through his hair. "I love you so much, it's sometimes hard to breathe," she said.

That's all he needed to hear.

As he stripped her of her panties, freed himself of his clothes, and entered her in one long, bone-shuddering stroke, he finally had the sensation that he'd truly come home.

Epilogue

LINCOLN WILLIAMS STOOD back and allowed his colleagues to explain what had taken place over the past day and a half. But as he watched Dari and Megan, he got the distinct impression the case wasn't the only area in which a breakthrough was made. If he wasn't mistaken, they'd managed to clear the debris keeping them apart and were now back to being a full-fledged couple. And he was never wrong.

Of course, it didn't hurt that Megan was wearing a rock any successful rap artist would be envious of. It didn't take a rocket scientist to predict wedding bells in their future.

He grimaced at the thought of his friend asking him to participate as a groomsman.

Jason took over the meeting, stepping up in front of the Lazarus crew.

"When Megan shared her theory, we split up. Linc here checked with his, um, contacts, as mysterious and powerful as they may be." Chuckles. "And I flew back to Florida to handle things from the sheriff's angle, while Megan and Dari stayed here to, um, coordinate things…"

More chuckles as everyone acknowledged what Linc had just been thinking.

Jason continued. "The FBI staked out McCain's place, making sure he stayed there until the sheriff could pick him up. The guy confessed almost immediately."

Megan took over. "Thankfully, this is the first time he's done something of this nature, but it's apparent that he'd hoped to do it again. When we happened across the girl's bike, we got too close for comfort and he panicked, bringing Finley back and acting like her rescuer."

Dominic shifted in one of the chairs. "Outside his obvious sick intentions, what had he planned to do with her?"

Linc shared a look with the other three, before Dari answered: "He wanted to marry her."

Groans and profanity filled the room.

Jason said, "Yeah, I think we all share the same sentiment. Which makes it a good thing Megan refused to accept his story and kept working the case. It seems he already had his next victim picked out. And this time, he just may have gotten it right."

They all fell silent as they digested that bit of news.

"So, what we're trying to say—" Dari cleared his throat "—is job well done, team!"

The group indulged in a bit of back patting, celebration obviously the name of the game.

Linc took that as his cue to leave the room, preferring not to participate. Truth was, his reaction was bittersweet. Sweet, in that Lazarus was growing into exactly what they'd hoped it might. Bitter in that there were two principal team members missing from the celebration—Eli Stark, who was a business partner and primary investor but preferred to remain silent in more ways than Linc was comfortable with, and Barry Lazaro, their late friend and inspiration.

Linc tried to shake off the dark thoughts, concentrating instead on the matter at hand, which happened to be a memo he'd received on his BlackBerry that morning—his FBI past had come back to haunt him in the form of one certain Billy Johnson, a serial bank robber he'd put behind bars two years ago. The man had made a daring jailbreak and was now wandering around a free man.

"Good job, Linc," Dominic said as he came out of the room.

He narrowed his gaze at the young agent, letting him know the hand he was about to use to pat him on the back was not only unwelcome, but may very well get him hurt.

Jason chuckled as he came to stand next to him, and Dominic moved on. "You know, these guys are scared spitless of you."

"Good." He cracked a grin.

Dari and Megan came out, his arm draped around

her shoulders. "You going to join us for a celebration lunch?"

Linc shook his head. "Pass."

"Well, if you change your mind, we'll be at The Barracks," Megan said.

The threesome left and Linc headed for the door. This case may have been put to bed, but he already had his sights set on the next bedroom. And a certain woman he was sure Billy "the Bank Robber" Johnson would try to seek out.

He intended to be there when he did…

* * * * *